Pa'l Otro Lado

and Other Tales of Bad Hombres & Nasty Women

by
Juan Ochoa

Lake Dallas, Texas

FIRST EDITION

Pa'l Otro Lado is a work of fiction. Names, characters, places, and incidents either are the products of the author's imagination or are used fictitiously. Any resemblance to actual events, locales, businesses, companies, or persons, living or dead, is entirely coincidental.

Requests for permission to reprint material from this work should be sent to:

Permissions
Madville Publishing
P.O. Box 358
Lake Dallas, TX 75065

Author Photograph: Benjamin Briones
Cover Art and Design: Edgar Torres

ISBN: 9781956440539 paperback, 9781956440546 ebook
Library of Congress Control Number: 2023936076

*I dedicate this book to my daughters,
Joy Monserrat, Rosa Desiree, and Amy.*

Contents

Quirina Moreno

¿Que paso? El tren por la villa, what else? Oh, you mean about that woman in the picture? Of course I know who she is; that's Quirina Moreno, she was my husband's grand-mother. Those things across her chest are cananas; they're for carrying bullets. She had to carry her bullets somewhere, didn't she? You want me to tell you about her? I don't know if I can do that. I never met her. People had a lot to say about Quirina Moreno, too much if you ask me but not enough if you ask others. I don't know much about anything and even less about Quirina, but I can tell you lo que dicen.

Quirina Moreno came from the other side of the sierra from Saltillo. Some say she was orphaned and had to follow goat trails down from the mountains all the way around Monterrey until she found her way to Los Ramones. Others say she was raised by a curandera who taught her all the secrets of both white and black magic, and that she had to leave her village because the people were afraid of her. I don't know if any of that is true. What I do know is that my father was there when she walked into town one day and didn't say a word to anyone until she passed through the doors of Domingo Cano's cantina.

That cantina was the jacal Luz Perez used to live in with Casimira Gonzalez before Domingo got his hands on it and turned it into a watering hole for cabrones. Casimira Gonzalez was Candida Carillo's cousin. Candida married Quirina's son, Chema, my suegro. I hadn't thought of that until now.

Bueno pues, Quirina walked right through those doors, and she didn't go to Domingo looking for work like other women had done before her. No, Quirina walked right up to the bar and laid her money down, just like a man, and ordered a beer. While everyone else was scraping their chins off the floor, Inez Cortina sprang from his chair –which was a pretty amazing thing because Inez Cortina didn't quicken his step for anyone—and crossed the bar to where Quirina was and told her that her money wasn't any good while he was around. They drank well into the night. Pues, eso dicen. What I do know for a fact is that the next morning the whole world saw Quirina sweeping the stoop in front of Inez's jacal—I must of heard my mother tell about it a hundred times.

There was a fuss about her taking up with Inez like that because she was a lot younger than him, and people tend to make something out of that. Everyone figured a man who owned a thousand goats couldn't stay single forever. And a young wife is always a man's first choice, especially when he can afford it.

The years passed and Quirina proved to be a big help when it came to tending goats and birthing babies. Not only her own babies; she helped in the birthing of pretty near every baby from the Hacienda San Antonio to el Rancho de Los Cantu. I'll bet there's not a roof in Los Ramones that doesn't keep the sun off of at least one rump that received its first slap from Quirina Moreno.

Oh sí, Quirina proved to be a big help to many around here. Of course not everyone appreciates like they should. Inez seemed content enough though, from what they say. Quirina always found the best pastures for his herds, and she gave him the handsomest children a man could ever lend his name to. First came Matilde with thick black locks and fair as the clearest of mornings. There wasn't a Christian around these parts who could pass Inez's patio without having to get off their cart and run their hands over Matilde's face so they wouldn't give her mal de ojo. Roll your eyes if you want to, but I've seen plenty a mother walk herself senseless all night with a crying baby who got the evil eye from some admirer who didn't think it necessary to touch the babe. You can believe what you like, but I know what I've seen.

Matilde was fine and beautiful. Then came Jose Maria –your father's Apa Chema and my suegro. Strong man, that Chema. You could place a kid goat's head in the palm of his hand and the next thing you'd see was goat's brain oozing out from between his stained fingers. He had mal de pinto; his hands and arms were spotted like a paint horse. That's why everyone called him *El Manos Pintas.* Some say it was from nerves that his hands got stained that way, but I heard that he had that discoloration since he was little, way before people started talking about his mother. Before Chema, of course, came poor Jose Pilar.

Quirina only gave Inez three children and there was plenty of talk about why they stopped at three. Anyone who's ever tried to raise a child should have known better pero ya vez. Anyway, those kids and the herds weren't enough to keep Quirina busy. No señor, not enough at all, she was brimming with what most men have hanging only as ornaments. That woman wasn't afraid to go anywhere at any time. It could be the middle of the night, and if you heard a galloping horse you could bet the whole hacienda that it was Quirina riding to help another soul come into the world. This might not seem like much now, but consider what the soldiers did to the women they found hiding in their homes and imagine what they would do to a woman riding out in el monte alone. Don't matter if they were Villistas or Federales. Putting everything a woman has in this world on a saddle and riding out in the middle of the night for someone else's child during a revolution is not something just anyone does. No, but it was what Quirina Moreno would do.

You see, she wasn't afraid of the night. She knew the monte too well for that. Every goat trail was as familiar to her as her own child's face. I've heard people tell about how she used to say, "if the horse doesn't mind the dark, then why should I?" She could go on these trails from one rancho to another in minutes when it took everyone else hours. And this is why the people came to her when women needed help giving birth. They knew Quirina would come and they knew she would be there quick. It was on one of these nights when she lost Pilar.

The soldiers were riding through Los Ramones—I don't remember if it was Villistas or Federals; it doesn't matter; they were all the same—giving every Christian the same choice, soldado or colgado. They hanged three men before the rest started to volunteer. Pilar couldn't have been more than fourteen when they took him away to fight. Quirina came home to find the news of her son being taken and she tore out after the pelotón with Inez's treinta-treinta.

She caught up to a small group of soldiers who had lagged behind. Quirina exchanged bullets with these men. Those who survived said they were attacked by a phantom that disappeared behind whiffs of gun smoke. One second she was to their left, then behind them, in front, all around

4

firing that rifle until she ran out of bullets. Those who could still run, did. But the story of la bruja Quirina ran faster. Quirina la mata hombres, the witch who could gallop through the monte under a rain of bullets and come out without a scratch.

People started to find more things to say about her. The train ran over one of Quirina's goats. It wasn't strange for people to lose animals on the tracks, but for it to happen to one of Quirina's goats was enough to keep the town talking for weeks. Enough for people to say she had thrown herself to el vicio. She started spending her evenings at Domingo's cantina. At first with Inez, then alone. People talked about that too. What? Of course Inez cared about her, pendejo. Sometimes the best way a man can show he cares about a woman is to leave her alone.

Fidencio Carrillo went up to Inez one day and said, "Quirina was drinking all night at Mingo's in a room full of men."

Fidencio said that Inez spit out his tobacco and said, "Well, I guess she must've been pretty thirsty."

Fidencio told the story to everyone he met ending it with, "That woman must have poor Inez embrujado." Quirina attacking soldiers and drinking alone in public scared people—mostly the men. But this didn't bother Quirina. She'd ride right through town, all dressed in black—she started wearing black after they took Pilar—her head held high. A group of men were standing around the plaza one day when Quirina was riding by and one of them thought it right to yell, "Vieja bruja."

Quirina turned her horse and rode right up to those men and just sat there on her horse. After a long time she said, "Just as I thought, puros cabrones." You ask anyone who was there that day and they'll tell you the same. Quirina didn't care if the whole world was watching; she always did what needed to be done.

So, people still called her when they needed her. She'd still go out and help deliver babies. She'd leave goat's milk and cheese for families who had none. If she slaughtered an animal, she'd send out meat to women who had lost their men to la Revolución. But people find gratitude a heavy thing to bear. It's always been easier to talk bad about someone than it is to be grateful for a favor they've done. At least it was when it came to Quirina. Then Patrocino Ochoa's baby died.

The child came early and wasn't positioned for birth. Quirina spent hours trying to massage the baby into place but it was no use. The child never got to take its first breath. Patrocino saw the baby, its skin cold and blue, and was sure it was brujeria. Quirina wrapped the baby in white cloth and stayed until they buried it the next morning.

Patrocino—no, he's no relation to you; he's an Ochoa from Los Herrera in the next county—he started saying it was Quirina who killed his baby. That she had tried her brujeria, and it went wrong. That it was a mal puesto. That's what they call it when a spell goes wrong, a mal puesto. And there was no shortage of people who added more hair to the pozole.

"How can a woman ride alone like that without being protected by the devil?"

"She shot it out with the soldados and didn't receive a scratch."

"Look how she has Inez, blind to everything she does."

All this talk was calentandole la cabeza a Patrocino. He could barely hear Quirina's name without going into a rage. He said she was a bruja. That she put spells on men and left them mute with her words. He didn't even respect the fact it was semana santa when he confronted Quirina.

Quirina and Inez were riding into town together. It was the end of lent and Quirina had a lamb stretched over her saddle on her way to the butcher's. Patrocino rode out blocking the way, and said to Quirina, "Is it true that bullets won't go into brujas."

Quirina said, "Pues, dicen." And Patrocino pulled his gun and shot her right between the eyes. Inez pulled his dagger and lunged at Patrocino but was only able to stab the horse as it ran past him. Patrocino rode that wounded animal till it died, but he got to the next county. And the sheriff wasn't the type to go chasing after a man all the way to the next county just for killing a woman.

Quirina fell face down. Her son, Chema—your great grandfather—ran out and turned her lifeless body over and burst out in shrieks when he saw the hole in her forehead.

All of Los Ramones came out to see them carry Quirina away; it was the first time the town's new stretcher had been used. No sooner than they had put her in the ground, the corridos started about how Quirina Moreno was killed por embrujar a los hombres. Pues eso dicen.

Apa Chema Falls in Love

Jose Maria Cortina bent down and rolled his mother's dead body over. He staggered back and nearly fell when the bullet hole in her forehead came into full focus. He stood looking down at her for a long time then wiped his nose with the back of his hand and collected his mother in his arms and carried her home so the women could clean and dress her for the funeral. Everyone had called him Chemita or el Manos Pintas because of the discoloring disease that had stained his hands and arms, but now, from this day forward, the people of Los Ramones would only address him as Don Chema, even though he was only eighteen years old.

His mother had been killed for bewitching men, and his father, stricken with unbearable grief, had decided to silently wait for his own death so he could join his beloved. So there was nothing left to do but become a man and care for his siblings and run the ranch. He could take solace in knowing that he was but one of many in the dusty little town who had received misery as an inheritance, but he knew that this type of consolation was for pendejos.

He threw himself to the task at hand. He grew his parents' already plentiful herd of goats to number in the thousands.

He planted three hundred hectares each of corn, sorghum, and beans and brought them in almost single-handedly. The land was rented, but only for three seasons; by then, men who had once rented him land now worked for him. He worked hard at building a name for himself under the withering heat from dawn till dusk, for what is a man if his name is not respected. This he believed more than anything else.

He was working in the fields when details of his brother Pilar's death were given to him. It was Gonzalo el Colorado who came sauntering up on his gray filly and stopping to run a heavy hand through his bright red locks before saying to Chema, "I know how they killed Pilar. The Federales. They captured him in Guanajuato. I met a man who said they had him tied to a wagon, pulling him along. At a stop, Pilar asked for water and the sergeant said, 'Give him milk.' The man told me that Pilar told him that he'd rather have a bullet. The sergeant pulled his gun and said, 'Granted.'"

"Who was this man who told you this?" Don Chema asked.

"A veteran of the battle for Celaya. He said Pilar's horse was shot from under him when he charged the lines to lasso a machine gun from its nest," Gonzalo said with pride.

"That sounds like something my big brother would do. He was not afraid of life, much less death."

Don Chema stood in the middle of his field watching Gonzalo ride off and taking in the news of his only brother's death as if it had just happened even though it had been many years since the Revolution had ended. A gorrión warbling on a mesquite branch struck a somber chord just as a lonely breeze slid down from the sierra through the fields and gently over Don Chema's shoulders and around his cheek till it caressed his lips. The coolness inflamed him, and he stretched his neck till it hung lingering long after the breeze had gone. His heart ached as much as his throat burned with dryness thinking of the thirst his brother must have felt before his death, and rage filled his chest as he fathomed the cold refusal of a quenching drink to a man being marched to his death. He mounted his horse and urged it toward town with a look of bitterness in his eyes. Doña Florinda was bringing in the eggs she collected from the coop and left the gate of her corral flung open blocking the trail. Don Chema jumped the four rails without breaking gallop. When the woman screeched in surprise, he reared his horse under a tree, grabbed hold of a solid branch, and kept the horse on its hind legs using the sheer power of his own legs to sustain the beast. When the woman dropped her basket of eggs, he roared with laughter, released the branch, and spurred the horse into a run without bothering to gather the reins.

Don Chema rounded the plaza at breakneck speed and made a beeline for the cantina's door. He pulled his horse into a slide when it was seemingly too late to avoid a collision, then just when the animal should have crashed into the wall, Don Chema whipped the steed around to turn and left a perfect arch painted with the horse's front hooves over the door of the cantina. Inside the cantina, Porfirio stood before Don Chema's table holding a tray with a glass and a bottle of tequila. He deposited the contents of the tray in front of Don Chema then stood still holding out the tray. Don Chema lugged a ten-peso coin onto the tray and said, "Tell me when that runs out."

But Porfirio did not move nor did he lower the tray. "Put your gun on the tray, Chema, and I'll keep it safe for you behind the bar."

"My gun feels fine tucked in my waist. I'll leave it there, thank you."

"But if the Federales come, or la rural, they will take it from you."

"No, Porfirio, the soldiers won't take my gun and neither will the mounted police. They have a right to try, but they will not take my gun," Don Chema said, filling himself a second glass of tequila.

The men sitting at nearby tables moved to the other end of the bar. Porfirio, seeing that for Don Chema the matter had been settled, retrieved another bottle of tequila from behind the bar and placed it on Don Chema's table. "That covers your ten pesos," he said.

Don Chema took his first of many drinks that day, but try as he might, he could not drown the sorrow that plagued his chest. Seeing Don Chema climb deeper and deeper into the bottle, the town figured it would not be long before he died at the hands of the Federales or from falling off that dun horse he rode so violently in a drunken state, but neither of those things happened.

One evening just as the last rays of the sun painted the lingering clouds bloody shades of red and purple, Don Chema saw a vision coming out of the Pesqueria, Juventina Cantu sat on her knees rocking back and forth in deep lament. Her raven hair was covered in a shawl of her own making. With the ends of this, she pressed her eyes to stop the steady flow of tears.

"What is wrong with you?" Chema asked from atop his horse.

Surprised, she yanked on her shawl and her hair cascaded down like crow's wings shining blue and black in the last rays of the day. "The man I was to marry was killed by the Federales," she said, like she was surprised to hear the words even though they had come out of her mouth.

"You'll be all right. I lost a brother at the hands of the Government," he said. And then without knowing why he added, "And my mother too."

Juventina looked up at him, fresh tears filling her eyes, "But you do not understand. I thought we would marry. I have sinned. I am no longer pure."

"Neither am I."

They stayed staring at each other for a long time captured in an unyielding web of desire. There was no simulation of seduction between the couple, only want and need that turned to blind lust. Juventina rose and stepped out of her dress like she was shedding a layer of death and then made her way into the Pesqueria River. Juventina Cantu's dark brown eyes gleamed as bright as the twilight that was casting shadows over the tree lined banks onto the river. Her caramel skin, thick and firm, glistened in streaking drops that flowed over and between the hills and valleys of her body in the fading light. He slid off his horse and out of his own clothes before she could blink. He stood pale against the coming night. His limbs like angel wings engulfed her and drew her into him. Her mouth, suddenly ravenous, bit at his chest, but finding this unyielding, moved hungrily to his neck and ears until descending over his welcoming lips.

She lived in a neighboring Rancheria, a half day's ride up river from his own farm, so it was not every day that he could see her, but when they did meet, their love was relentless. The rippling waters, the croaking frogs, and chirping crickets serenaded their love making. Their heaving bodies bathed in the moonlight and for hours the world was theirs and no one else's. In Juventina's arms, Don Chema was lost and he was in no hurry to find his way out. His calloused hands turned to silk as he ran his fingers over her quivering body. On the banks of the Rio Pesqueria, he explored all that she was, and she gave herself unflinchingly. And so it went for years.

As time passed, their encounters strayed from the banks of the Pesqueria. He took her in the corn field where the maize stood like green sentries shielding them from prying eyes. He met her in the barn where the bleating of the herded goats blended with pleasure filled sighs and climatic moans. Behind the corrals, where his dun horse pawed the ground and pranced and nickered giddy as the lovers, he leaned her against the rails and lifted her flowing ruffles so he could take her from behind. He offered no more than what stood before her, which she took. Their bond did not need for hallowed words or state drawn contracts. They belonged to each other and it did not matter who did or did not know about their commitment. Then Don Chema saw Cándida Carrillo.

She stepped out of the monte into a clearing that opened up on the trail that Don Chema was riding just as the wind peeled back a cloud to allow a single beam of moonlight to dance over Cándida's slender frame. Don Chema's horse shied, but he sat back on the reins and spurred the beast into a full circle with one back hoof firmly planted in the ground. Collecting himself on his mount, Don Chema eyed the girl who stood staunch and firm facing the panting stallion.

"What are you doing out at this hour?" he asked. He had been upset earlier that he had traded a night with Juventina for the warmth of a tequila bottle, but now he wondered if this was another turn of fate like when he had chosen to go into town for what now seemed like no other reason other than to be there at the precise moment Patrocino shot his mother from her horse. Chema had his doubts about God. He had never seen him. But he knew that there were powers that toyed with men.

"You ride well for a borracho," Cándida said ducking under the horse's head to take up the trail.

"That's no concern of yours," he said, kicking up the horse to ride next to her. "I asked you what you are doing out here."

"I came to deliver Chabela's baby," she said matter-of-factly. "Aren't you old enough to know that babies are like drunks? They don't care about time or place when the urge strikes them."

"You're a partera?"

"I am."

"My mother delivered babies," he said aloud before realizing it.

"I know. She taught me."

Don Chema brought his horse around to face Cándida and studied her face in the moonlight. "Whose daughter are you?" he asked at length.

"I'm Cándida Carrillo," she said, grabbing hold of the horse's bridle.

"You're Carrillo's daughter? He only has little girls." Don Chema slid off his mount to face Cándida.

"Little girls grow up," she said so softly that Chema thought her words might have been the wind blowing down from the sierra. He stepped forward, and she did not move back. "It's dangerous to be out, even if you're bringing souls into the world."

"You're out," she said, staring straight into his eyes.

"I'm a man," he said, wrapping his arm around her waist and pulling her in, crushing her body into his.

"Are you a man, Chema?" She asked dryly. "Can you show respect, or do you just take?" Her words hit Don Chema like a bucket of ice water and in that instant he was more sober than the day before he had tasted his first drop of tequila. He released his hold and made a big show over gathering up his horse's reins.

Before he could turn to face her again, she said, "Real men see women in the light of day, in front of God and everyone else, before they try to put their arms around them at night."

He started to stammer through an apology but a snapping twig made him stop. He looked back to where she had been standing only to find moonlight caressing the branches of a mesquite tree. She was gone. He knew where she lived and the trails that led there. He could catch up to her. But he didn't do that.

The next day, the men of Los Ramones dragged their tired bodies into the cantina and drank in bewildered silence. Fidencio, the grave digger, sat with his head cradled in one hand while he strummed the table with his mud-caked fingers—his mescal untouched. When Porfirio, just to have something to do, came by to wipe down the table and ask if he wanted another shot, Fidencio slammed his hand down and exclaimed, "He was sitting there, on Carrillo's front porch, with her. I saw him. I saw him just as plain as I'm seeing you right now."

Gonzalo el Colorado leapt up from his barstool and said, "Damn it. I knew it wasn't just me. He was there. Sitting there, across from Cándida. His hat in hand." He shook his own sweat-stained sombrero at the half dozen pairs of eyes that stared back at him from under bushy dark eyebrows and glistening foreheads. The men gathered in the cantina filled the room with excited table slapping murmurs and teeth sucking retorts as they slid and jockeyed their chairs around Fidencio to share their testimonies.

Fidencio turned and pointed a bent finger at Porfirio, which he then turned on the rest of the bar and said, "He rode that dun horse of his right past the cemetery and I yelled at him, '¿A donde vaz en este calor, Don Chema?' and he says without even turning to see who called him, 'I'm going to ask Carrillo if I can visit with his daughter, Cándida.' I nearly fell into the grave I was digging. And I would have stayed there too if the curiosity hadn't been so much."

15

The men slapped their dusty knees and crumpled the wings of their brittle hats and shook their heads as they listened. The man everyone called La Pasajera said, "He wasn't lying, either. I saw him when I passed Carrillo's place. He waited just outside the fence till Carrillo himself opened the gate for him and called Cándida out of the house."

Carlos Cantu from El Refugio shouted, "He'll ruin her like he did Juventina."

Carlos stood with his glass before his stubbly chin and declaimed, "We all know what he's been doing with Juventina for years now. But at least he never brought the family into it. To use a woman after speaking with her father is a mockery."

"Don't compare goats to horses," Porfirio said, pouring himself a shot after setting up the room with another round. Porfirio sipped from his glass then placed a foot on a chair in front of Fidencio and leaned in and said, "Have any of us here present ever known Don Chema not to keep a promise?" Porfirio leaned back and let his words sink into the room. The men all agreed that whether it be a fair deal or a beating, no one could remember a time when Don Chema didn't deliver on his promise.

"No," Fidencio said, looking past Porfirio to Carlos. "There is no joking around with Don Chema. He paid me for digging his mother's grave even before I could sharpen my pick. Then he buried her himself and wouldn't let me do nothing but watch while he did it." This bit of history set all the heads in the room to solemn nodding and even Carlos had to recognize that Don Chema was a man of verguenza.

Porfirio, confident that his point had been backed up sufficiently, continued his reasoning aloud, saying, "He sat there, on her porch, in broad daylight. You all saw that, right?"

The room affirmed the testimony with nods and shots of mescal and much elbowing. Sure now that he had the room

16

teetering, Porfirio stroked his chin whiskers and announced, "I'll go you one better. He sent over fifty kilos of rice and fifty kilos of beans over to Carrillo's house right after he left Cándida on the porch." The room erupted into a collective gasp as men turned to face each other in stunned befuddlement. "Hipolito Ramos carried the sacks over in his cart. Watered his horses right outside on his trip back." Porfirio stood in the middle of the gasping group raising his hands to silence them. "Gentlemen, the worry here is not for Cándida's virtue. She seems to have taken care of that on her own. What should concern us all is that," he paused to cast his stare into every eye in the room, "it is obvious that the Cortina men have been cursed to marry witches."

The sacks of rice and beans were meant to support Cándida till she and Don Chema could marry, which they did within a few months of their encounter in the monte. From the moment he left Cándida that day at her father's house, he saw to her every need. Every morning, he left at her feet a four-liter bucket of fresh milk and a basket of eggs, and he also filled her arms with a sack of ground maize for the tortillas. When he finished making the biggest jacal la Hacienda San Antonio had ever seen, Don Chema Cortina married Cándida Carrillo and had four sons: Barbarito, Nicolas, Vicente, and Aniceto.

The penultimate child, Vicente, Cándida brought home one day before dawn. She had been out attending to the young school teacher the county had sent the previous year. The fledgling educator refused to tell her mother who the father of the child was, and in a desperate panic, the mother had tried to salvage her daughter's honor by attacking the newborn with the center balance of a wagon rigging. Cándida was cutting the umbilical cord when the woman tried to kill the child. She was barely able to shield the innocent baby and was herself hit on the back enough times to drop her to the floor. Over the frightened shrieks of the babe, Cándida was able to convince the school teacher's mother that she could take her daughter's child and no one would be the wiser. Cándida would raise the child as her own. Did he not have light skin like hers? Weren't Cándida and her daughter almost the same age? Cándida was out the door and lost on the trail to all but herself and the swaddled child before the woman could answer. Don Chema was drinking coffee in the dark when she came in with the newborn in her arms. He traded his cup for the child and looking down at the pink face staring up at him from the folds of the blanket asked, "Is it a girl?" He frowned a little when she shook her head and sighed. "Too bad," he said. "We only have boys."

On the nights he returned from work to find the pots cold in his home, Don Chema marched his boys into town to the only restaurant, Lupita's, and sat his brood down at any table the boys fancied whether it was occupied or not. As long as the talk stayed behind his back, Don Chema ignored the tongue wagging his critics did about a married man and his children eating in a restaurant while his wife was out riding alone to tend to someone else's child. Porfirio, the bartender, tried to bring up the gossip once in conversation but Don Chema stopped him cold, saying, "If words were bullets, we'd all die like cowards with holes in our backs." That's why Don Chema didn't do anything but snort and dust off his hat on his knee when the gossip about Juventina's wedding reached him.

He only watched when Usebio, the town idiot, stretched his lanky legs and swiveled his melon head on his narrow shoulders as he marched past Don Chema's field leading a painted calf to be slaughtered for Juventina's nuptial feast.

One day, as he was bending his body to face a sudden gust blowing down from the mountains of Saltillo, Juventina passed in a wagon accompanied by her parents and all her brothers and sisters on her way to get fitted for her wedding dress. His back got rigid and he followed the wagon's progress with his eyes for as long as he could. He even paced out to the middle of the road and stood there as if somehow he could see Juventina through the dust kicked up by the wagon.

The days that passed before the wedding, Don Chema spent riding the monte for strays. He was herding a cow and her calf away from a muddy bank along the Pesqueria when he heard the church bells. The sound came faint at first like water dripping off the roof of his jacal after a rain. As he pointed the dun horse toward town, the sound of the chiming bells grew stronger but not strong enough to cover the sound of his own beating heart. There were fireworks exploding in the air above the mesquites and palo blancos that lined the plaza near the church. The service was over. The crowd gathered on the steps of the chapel, their faces illuminated with laughter, and began to cheer as Juventina and her new husband emerged from the church under a hail of rice and confetti. Don Chema saw the white satin ribbons that were braided in her hair flutter in the wind as her new husband lifted her by the waist into an awaiting buggy pulled by a blaze-faced black gelding. The man settled himself next to his new bride and steered the buggy out of town. Don Chema passed the couple and doffed his hat and opened his mouth as if in greeting but the words could only come out as a guttural roar that startled the black gelding pulling the buggy. Don Chema slapped his own horse on either shoulder with the reins and dug his spurs in with fury while Juventina sat, mouth agape, grabbing hold of the buggy seat as her new husband tried to steady the shying gelding. The animal jetted forward and Don Chema leaned in urging it to go faster. He set course for the church and scattered the crowd gathered on the steps. The horse made a clattering leap onto the cantera tiled patio in front of the church, sending the animal sliding toward the open door before Chema sat down on the reins, allowing the horse to gather its footing and continue its charge. He pulled the beast around at the last minute and painted an arch over the church's doors with his horse's front hooves just like he had done over the cantina years earlier.

Some of the onlookers were making their way back up the steps when Chema sent them running again as he lunged his horse back toward Juventina's buggy. He reached the couple in a flash of dust and horse sweat despite the new husband whipping the gelding into a gallop. He grabbed Juventina by the elbow and pulled her near till her ear was covering his mouth. He galloped next to the fleeing buggy with his mouth pressed into Juventina's ear till the buggy reached the cement slab that served as a bridge over the Pesqueria. Only God and Juventina know what Chema told her that day.

Not a week after the wedding, Chema was riding the banks of the Pesqueria just as the sun was saying its last farewells to a waxing moon. He rode out of a gully as Juventina's bronzed body was parting the lapping waters, stepping over the slick rocks to the shore where her clothes lay waiting. Drops of water streaked down and over her breasts like angel tears. Chema slid off his horse and wrapped her in his arms. Their mouths, hungry for each other, met and parted as they discovered new pieces of flesh to kiss and devour. He was in her and she enveloped him like darkness does the predawn. He rocked and thrust till he felt her shudder under him, and he himself exploded in passion. As he stared down at Juventina's half-closed eyes, a faint breeze blew down from the sierra and caressed his heaving frame; it scurried up his chest till it swirled around his flush lips and pulsing ears. The breeze lingered and melted in with the sounds of chirping crickets and buzzing cicadas that serenaded their love making. His blood churned like the untamed river that flowed near them as he felt his desire for Juventina grow yet again. Her breath broke and heaved with acceptance of every touch and the night came in dark and cool and joined them in desire. Their voices and pleasure blended with the sounds of the night and they were lost in each other's arms—so much so that they didn't notice that God was watching.

To Kill a Compadre

The affair between Don Chema and Juventina went on for thirty-five years. At their age, it was a bigger wonder that they still had the energy to get to their not so secret meetings than it was that they had lasted so long as lovers. Each had made a separate life that they were desperately loyal to. They both had married someone they loved and had had children and raised families and lived to see grandchildren. And in different circumstances, they might have had all these things together had it not been for the fact that although they did love each other, neither liked anything the other said or did.

Throughout all this time, their secret passed from mouth to mouth and generation to generation in alternating mentoring tones of asi es la vida, "such is life." And each wagging tongue took the news however it best suited them. Chema's son Aniceto and Juventina's son Santana became the best of friends when the latter was too small to leave alone or trusted to the care of anyone else. Chema would bring his son Cheto and leave the two playing while the grownups otherwise entertained themselves. As the need to bring them grew less, Cheto and Santana sought out their own ways of meeting and continuing their bond. They grew up like brothers and thought of each other as such even after they were able to figure out why their mother and father used to bring them to play with each other so much. As young men starting their own families, Cheto and Santana took to rustling cattle and opened up a carneceria together that quickly went bankrupt because they gave away all the meat in their butcher shop on credit. After this enterprise failed, they decided to become compadres and Santana stood as padrino when Cheto's second oldest son, Julio, got his first haircut.

It could be argued that everything would have been fine, and many have done just that, if Santana had not taken the job as foreman at the hacienda San Antonio. It was there that don Valencia first started poisoning him. But it could also be said that things happen for a reason and sins and good deeds, especially those involving people who love each other, never go unpunished.

Cheto had rounded up a few strays and drove them back to the hacienda as a favor to his compadre Santana. He saw don Valencia in the dusk. Santana, mounted on the dun gelding they had broken together, stood next to him. Cheto thought it best to push the cattle ahead and be on his way. He knew don Valencia was a man who could not resist talking in slights and faints so why even give him the opportunity. He waved his hat at the pair and reeled his horse and trotted back through the big gate and down the road.

"Look how he mocks you," don Valencia said to Santana. "He leaves those strays and waves his hat at you like you were a child who needs to be shown how to do his job."

Santana sat back in his saddle looking at his boss. "Do you think I need lessons on how to do my job?"

"You wouldn't be my foreman if I did." Don Valencia spat. "But I wasn't raised by a shameless man either. Be raised by a coyote and you'll learn to howl."

"Cheto is my compadre and don Chema is like a father to me."
Valencia laughed and turned his horse to leave but not before saying, "of course he's like a father to you. He's sleeping with your mother."

The words burned Santana's face which was bad enough, but they also did something much worse. They planted a seed that don Valencia cultivated and groomed and made bloom into tragedy.

"It's your mother's honor that I worry about," don Valencia said, pouring Santana another shot of tequila in his office. "It's strange that I worry more about these things than her own son. But you are young and do not realize what type of a scoundrel Jose Maria Cortina really is."

"He's never been nothing but good to me," Santana said, wiping his hand over a sweaty brow before sucking in more tequila.

"Your poor mother made a foolish mistake when she was but an innocent child who fell for the lies and promises of an ox. And ever since he's been holding it over her, threatening to expose her if she does not relent to his bestial desires," don Valencia said soothingly. "Why even I fell for the deceitful Chema when I sold him the land on the fringe of the hacienda. He coyly agreed to pay an exorbitant price for what he led me to believe was worthless land. He never told me he would dig his own wells and turn it into a garden."

Santana looked up at his boss teary eyed and under a sweaty brow. Expose his mother, he thought. To what? Cheating out of land that is as demanding as life itself. How? He did not understand these things that Valencia was putting in his head. He buried his face in his hands and his whole body shook.

"You worry about your compadre, don't you Santana?" Don Valencia pulled a bundle out of a drawer and then took

24

the chair opposite his foreman. "That's just a testament of how much a better man you are than him."

Don Valencia put the bundle on the desk in front of Santana. He unfolded a layer of cloth to reveal a brand new Colt .38 Super. Santana's eyes got wide and he had to lick his lips before he could talk again.

"That's a 1911 model, isn't it? My compadre, Cheto and I have been wanting to buy..." Santana's words trailed off. He reached for the gun but stopped to look at his boss to see if it was ok.

"Go ahead, Santana, pick it up," don Valencia said smiling. "I got it for you. I want you to have it."

Santana was overcome. He eagerly reached for the Colt. He palmed the gun and checked its weight. He worked the slide and made sure there was no bullet in the chamber. Finally, he looked down the sights and pulled the trigger. "Mother of God. What a fine weapon. Why, a man with a gun like this need not be afraid of anything or anyone."

"That's right, Santana. With a gun like this, everyone will have to respect you. Even that sorry excuse for a man, Chema Cortina."

Santana swallowed hard and set the gun back on the table. "Jose Maria Cortina carries a gun. Maybe not like this one, but it fires, and in his hands, it's deadly."

Don Valencia pushed the gun closer to Santana. He got up and strolled around the desk until he was behind his foreman. He bent over and spoke in hushed tones into Santana's ear. "No one would blame you for just walking up to Chema Cortina and shooting him dead on the spot. He has dishonored you and your family for long enough. You could wait for him where the river bends and the road veers. You don't even have to announce your intentions. You could shoot Chema and restore your mother's honor before that worthless excuse for a man could even draw his pistol."

Don Valencia spoke to Santana like that for a long time.

Jose Maria Cortina rode his horse slowly down the road, his eyes locked on the tracks he had been following for more than a kilometer. The tracks belonged to Santana. Don Chema had first noticed them when he took the road after meeting with Juventina. He could tell that Santana had spurred his horse and run far ahead of him by the way the hooves dug deep into the dirt. The tracks grew longer which told him that the horse had begun to slow into a soft gallop. All these things he could tell just by studying the ground, but what he did not understand is what caused Santana to be so deliberate in staying ahead of him. Now the tracks left the road, and even a blind man could tell that the brush had been cut by horse and rider toward the big mesquite that grew at the bend in the river. Don Chema could see Santana's horse standing at the river's edge but there was no sign of the rider. He stood in his stirrups to survey the land and was nearly knocked off his mount by a whizzing bullet. Chema reeled his horse and sank his spurs into the animal causing it to rear up. Chema pulled his .32 caliber Smith and Wesson and squeezed off two shots before taking to the brush. From there he called out to Santana.

"Have you been smoking marijuana, boy? It's me. Chema."

Two more shots came from behind the mesquite before Santana shouted, "I'm going to kill you Jose Maria."

"I'll see you face down in the dirt first, huerco pendejo. But tell me why you want to kill me."

"No te hagas pendejo, Chema. I know what you did to my mother."

"I've never hurt your mother. Have you gone mad? I would never hurt her."

Santana came out from behind the mesquite firing his weapon till it was empty. While he fumbled to change clips,

Chema emptied his own gun but only to spook Santana's horse. Santana turned to watch his ride splash across the river. Don Chema was mounted and down the road in the opposite direction before Santana could get off another shot.

Don Chema came in at a full gallop to the yard of the big jacal. His son Cheto was lying lazily on the porch with his sombrero covering his eyes. Cheto rose with a start to see his father come bounding off his horse and rush into the adobe house only to come out a moment later carrying a Remington ten shot .22 caliber rifle.

"¿Que paso, Apa?"

"Your fool compadre fired on me, that's what happened. Right there where the big mesquite throws shade on the river."

"My compadre? Santana? Why would he shoot at you?"

"He said because of his mother."

Cheto picked up his hat and slapped it across his leg and began pacing the porch. "I knew something like this would happen. Why do you keep seeing her?"

Don Chema stared at his son searching for something to say, his whole body aquiver. When his breath had come back to him Don Chema simply said, "I can't help it."

Cheto wanted to scream. His eyes filled with tears and he bit down hard on his own knuckles till his head quit swimming. Don Chema put a comforting hand on his son's shoulder and both men hung their heads and sobbed.

Cheto wiped his nose with the back of his hand and said to his father, "You're not going to kill my compadre."

"Well I'm not going to let him kill me either." Chema pulled the rod out of the rifle's sleeve and dropped .22 shells into it till no more would fit. "I've done nothing to Santana."

"You are with his mother," Cheto said in almost a whisper, "and it is what it is."

"No mijo. It *is* what we make it to be and nothing more.

27

What's changed? I bet it's that sonofabitch Valencia that's poisoned his mind."

While Cheto and his father spoke on the porch, Santana had made his way back to don Valencia's office. Don Valencia looked at his foreman and knew that the young man had failed in his task. "It's ok," Valencia said, taking out a square tin with a red cross painted on it from his desk. "You just got a little nervous." He pulled out a vile and a syringe. He began to fill the syringe with an oily liquid as he spoke softly to Santana.

"This is morphine. This is what the gringos used to beat the Kaiser. One shot of this and you'll be able to shoot Chema down in the street like the dog that he is."

"He knows it was me who shot at him. I told him why. He'll be ready."

"And it won't matter." Don Valencia reached over and stretched out Santana's bare arm then plunged the needle into a vein. Santana watched as his blood blossomed into a macabre flower in the syringe then disappeared as a wave of warmth covered him from head to toe. His body began to itch and everywhere he scratched exploded in ecstasy. He felt his heartbeats coming in waves and although he could barely keep his eyes open, he felt energy well in his chest like he had never felt before. He left the office and mounted his horse again and headed out the big gate. His brother Facundo was running up the road toward him. "Santana, everyone is saying that you shot at don Chema down by the river. Tell me it's not true."

"It's true," Santana said. Facundo trotted behind his brother till they reached the cantina where he convinced Santana to stop for a drink.

Poncho, the boy who swept the cantina, came running up to the jacal grande with the news that Santana was at the cantina telling everyone that he was going to have El Manos Pintas for dinner.

"What did Porfiro say when he heard that?" Chema asked the boy.

"He said don't be too sure that Chema won't make a meal out of you."

"Well it's done," Chema said to his son. "Everyone knows and he'll have to act and so will I." Chema pulled out his revolver and checked the cylinder to make sure it was full. "You have to make sure only to lose a fight for lack of balls not bullets."

Cheto didn't have time to answer when they both saw Santana riding toward them with his brother Facundo trotting a ways behind. Cheto picked up the Remington rifle and stayed his father from leaving the porch with an outstretched palm. "Let me talk to him."

Cheto walked out into the road and covered the distance between him and his compadre with deliberate steps.

"What do you want, Cheto?" Santana asked.

Cheto noticed how he was called by his name and not compadre. Shouldering the .22, he looked up at Santana and said, "I want you to shoot at me like you shot at my father."

Santana reeled his horse and pulled the .38 Super. Cheto brought down the rifle and began to fire. The first three shots hit the horse in the neck causing the animal to stagger and make the most horrible sounds. Cheto's children came flooding out of the house to see what was the matter. Little Julio was at the gate when he saw his father fire four bullets into Santana. Santana winced with pain and dropped the .38. Facundo bent over to pick the gun up and Cheto fired what was left in the .22 at Facundo only meaning to scare him off but Facundo's hand went to his side to stop a sudden spray of blood from leaking out even more. Santana fell face first into the dirt struggling to breathe.

Don Chema bent over Santana's body and rolled him over saying, "This is how I wanted to see you hijo de tu chingada madre."

Cheto walked back to the jacal where his son Julio was standing and ordered the boy to hitch up the cart. "You have to take your padrino home to his family."

Chema stood facing his son. Cheto swallowed hard and said, "I've killed my compadre."

"Don't you ever speak those words again to anyone." Don Chema took Cheto by the shoulders and said, "I shot Santana. You were nowhere near here because you were on your way to find work in the United States."

A few hours later, Cheto was sitting in a box car heading north. There were other men in the car with him. They were smoking marijuana and drinking mescal. A nervous man sat fidgeting next to Cheto. "All those men smoking over there owe lives. Killers, every one of them."

Cheto looked at the man and then at the others who were smoking. He got up and reached out for the marijuana cigarette and filled his lungs even though he had never smoked before. He let the smoke out slowly before asking, "Does anyone know how long it will take us to get to the United States?"

A few of the men laughed. One from the group took the cigarette back from Cheto and said dryly, "This train is taking us to hell, but you can call it the United States if you want."

Another man said, "Yeah, we're all heading to where there is only work and sweat."

"That's what I told him," said the man who now held the smoldering weed. "We're all going to hell on this train. Tell us amigo, what brings you to hell?"

Cheto took the cigarette back and tugged on it till his

head began to swim. After a while he said, "I'm going to hell because my father loved a woman."

The men in the box car exploded with laughter.

Someone lifted the bottle of mescal and said, "Falling in love with a woman is terrible. That's the worst thing a man can do in this life."

The New Suit

"¿Que ira a pasar?" Quina sighed as she looked out the window of her adobe kitchen. "Mira a Inez y Julio, cuñada, playing there like two pups. I could swear I was looking at someone else's sons."

Hortencia stopped kneading dough to peer out the doorway at her nephews frolicking in the patio. "They're just excited about Julio's birthday," she said with a tired smile. "Todo el mundo se hace amigos when there's a fiesta."

"Amigos mis chiches," Quina chuckled. "They're content because of where their father is taking Julio after the cena."

"¿Sí, cuñada?" Hortencia's eyes widened. "Mí viejo told me that he is going with Cheto and Julio to Caderyta tonight after we all eat. I don't care what my viejo says, twelve is just too soon." Hortencia sunk her fist into a mound of masa and said, "It must be hard for you to see two sons ya hombres."

"Julio, you and Inez stay out of the jacal grande; don't even think of touching those clothes with your dirty hands. I'm not going to tell you again," Quina scolded her sons from the window then turned to face her sister-in-law. "It'll be Nico's turn to take your Chemita to dance with those pinche viejas in a couple of months."

"Don't remind me Cuñada," Hortencia sighed. "Let me enjoy my hijito while I can, even if it's just for a couple of months more."

Quina stoked the coals and greased her comal then started pinching off bits of dough to pat into little cakes called gorditas. Between the grinding of the chocolate and the kneading of the dough there had been numerous breaks to delve into the mysteries surrounding the stupidity of men and their incessant need to search the streets for what they hardly used at home. Hortencia's aid had been a welcomed pause from Quina's ordinarily solitary chores, but now she was starting to feel the pressure of the sun climbing over her kitchen as she thought of the men working the campo and tending the herds on an empty stomach.

"I'm going to send Inez to the fields with Cheto and Nico's lunch," Quina said. "Julio can take primo Lucio his lunch down to the river and watch the goats for him while he eats."

"Oh no, Cuñada, don't do that," Hortencia said. "My Chemita and Nicky will be here soon, we'll send them. It would be such a shame to make Julio do errands on his birthday."

"I'll only wait for as long as it takes me to pack the men their lunch," Quina said. "You know how necios men get when they're hungry and want their food."

Just outside the adobe kitchen, Inez and Julio stopped play wrestling and stretched out side by side under the shade of a mesquite tree.

"Do you think he'll take me?" Julio asked, his eyes sparkling brighter than the sun filtering through the mesquite branches.

"He took me last year when I turned twelve," Inez said, smiling warmly remembering the night his father took him to Cadereyta to dance in the cantinas. "Parecian cabras, there were women all over the place, standing in doorways, walking up and down the sidewalk, sitting on cars..." Inez rolled over, propping his arm up under his head so that he faced his little brother. "Everywhere you turned you ran into some fancy smelling woman with more plaster on her face than the church in Los Ramones."

Julio sat up. "But what are they doing in the streets?"

Inez hugged his stomach and began kicking his feet, giggling. "Nothing," he said. "I tell you they're out there like a herd of goats just milling around waiting for someone to come round them up."

Julio giggled too, nervously. "Do they say anything? I mean, can you talk to them? Are they friendly?"

"They chatter and squawk louder than a flock of uracas," Inez sat up. "All they do is stagger around, talking to themselves like locas until they run up on someone to hug and call chulo and guapo."

"I don't believe they just start hugging you just like that in the street in front of everybody," Julio said. "What if someone's mother saw you or something?"

"Nobody's mother is on the streets of Cadereyta," Inez said. "Even the women you see there aren't from Cadereyta. They just come up from Monterey or San Pedro to make money dancing and then they go back home and act like saints."

"Well, I know they don't dance out in the streets."

"The drunk ones do," Inez said smiling broadly. "Dad will probably take you to tio Julio's place, which will be even better for you because tio Julio will most likely make one of his girls dance with you for free. You're named after him and all."

"Where did my tio Julio meet all these women?" Julio asked.

"He didn't meet them," Inez said. "Solitas vienen, they just come into his place and line up on the wall waiting for someone to ask them to dance. They have to pay part of what they make to tio Julio," Inez scratched his head. "I guess for the electricity it takes to run the jukebox. It's twenty cents for every dance, but tio Julio has the jukebox rigged so the song only lasts a minute and then se chingo el veinte." Both boys roared with laughter.

"Twenty cents for only a minute dance," Julio said. "It doesn't seem like much of a bargain."

"Find yourself a tall one and hug her real tight," Inez said with a wink. "See where your head goes and then come back and tell me it wasn't worth twenty cents. Besides, if you dance five songs in a row for a peso they let you dance an extra song for free, el pilón."

"And what about when you're dancing?" Julio ran his nervous fingers through his hair. "What do you talk about when you're dancing?"

Inez thought for a moment. "I spent most of the night apologizing for stepping on their feet," he said. "But after a while I figured out if you squeeze them tight enough you don't have to move as much."

"What if no one wants to dance with me?" Julio asked anxiously.

"Everybody gets to dance, even Beto el prieto," Inez said, starting to get a bit annoyed at his little brother's lack of confidence. "You'll have money." Inez tugged at his brother's shirt. "And it's not like you're going in your T-shirt and huaraches."

Julio's eyes got wide with excitement imagining Beto el prieto, the dark skinned, buck-toothed merchant's son, who was the butt of every ugly joke imaginable, not getting turned down for a dance. If Beto could find a dance partner,

Julio thought to himself, he could too. Besides, in all the talk of viejas and dancing he had forgotten the fact that he would be sporting his new suit that evening. It wouldn't be long before his mother would make him bathe and change into his new conjunto she had bought for him in Monterrey. Julio remembered how his younger siblings, and even Inez, had gasped with envy when his mother tore open the brown wrapping to reveal Julio's new suit. Light blue pleated slacks cuffed at the hem. A matching sky blue guayabera trimmed with embroidered pleats that formed six delicate ridges running down either side, held together and accented with bone-colored buttons running down the chest and centered on each of the four pockets. Such fine apparel was seldom seen in Los Ramones aside from the times the county clerks came to town from Caderyta to collect the taxes for the school. Julio pictured himself strutting around his uncle's cantina in his new suit, stopping and extending his hand to some woman who was much taller than him then losing himself in her softness. And this muñequita de porcelana would be so pleased to be dancing with such a finely dressed young man that she wouldn't even notice that he could only do the box step. Julio checked the kitchen window to assure himself that his mother was sufficiently occupied and was just about to solicit his older brother's aid in sneaking into the armoire where the new clothes were stored when he heard his cousins Chemita and Nicky coming towards their house leading a colt.

"Hola Inez, Feliz cumpleaños Julio," Chemita held up the lead rope. "I brought my potrillo so we could ride him before our mothers start serving the merienda."

"Y qué padre primo," Julio said, trotting over to greet his cousins.

"At least he'll be doing something other than asking me

pendejadas," Inez said, joining the group. "You should hear Julio primo, '¿Y qué dicen, y cómo bailan?'"

"What do you think I came over for?" Chemita chuckled. "There's still two months and ten days left before my birthday and my chance to go."

"Andale Inez," Julio teased, "tell us one more time how to conquer women in Caderyta so we can be like you."

Inez scooped up little Nicky and sat him on the horse and said, "Maybe Nicky and I should ride this harp over to Caderyta and leave you two here to figure things out for yourself."

"Yo ya conozco," Nicky said, wiping snot from his nose with his bare hand.

"He's not lying," Chemita said. "My Apa took him once when he was in a hurry and Nicky wouldn't get off the truck. Apa says he slept most of the time they were there, but at least he can say he went."

"What did you see, primito?" Julio asked Nicky.

Nicky bunched his chubby fingers together and exclaimed, "Chingos de viejas."

"I'm hearing every word you say, Nicolas," Hortencia called out from the kitchen.

"No fui yo Ama," Nicky said then began to bawl.

Chemita and Julio were rigging a bridle out of the lead rope while Inez made sure Nicky didn't bawl himself off the horse when their mothers called to them from the kitchen doorway.

"Chemita, you need to run the comida out to the men," Hortencia said, wiping her hands on her apron. "Hurry so you can come back and we can serve the gorditas de harina and chocolate."

Little Nicky's face broke into a wide smile, "Uhm, I love gorditas."

"You'll love the skinny ones too once you get older," Quina said playfully to her sobrino. "Julio, you need to go and take your bath now para que puedas estrenar tu traje nuevo."

While Julio enjoyed the warm water and creamy suds his mother had prepared for him, his uncle Lucio paced irritably up and down the banks of the Pesqueria. The sun burning the nape of his neck did little to warm the hungry knot that was tightening in his stomach. Lucio had decided since he had not been brought his lunch, he would not allow any of the cabras he was tending to drink from the river, whacking any goat bold enough to stray towards the watery bank across the back with the 30-30 he carried. Lucio had herded them into a break in the bordo and had been able to contain them there until a few of the more restless goats started finding their way over the flanking ridges. This infuriated Lucio even more, causing him to pick up river rocks and hurl them at the bleating strays. But this only frightened the rest of the herd and the goats began pouring out of the makeshift corral in even greater numbers. Lucio ran into what remained of the huddled herd and clubbed a kid goat to its knees. The chivito rose on shaky legs, its incessant bleating annoying Lucio to a higher level of rage. He even went as far as to chamber a round and would have fired on the helpless beast had not the sound of Chemita breaking through the monte with his horse in tow forced him to redirect his irritation.

"¿Donde chingados has estado?" Lucio demanded. "You've been goofing off with that pinche caballo instead of bringing me my lunch like you were supposed to, you spoiled little brat." Lucio held the rifle in one hand by the breach and waved the barrel under the horse's muzzle, "I've got a good mind to shoot this mule of a horse no mas pa' quitarte lo chiflado."

"No, don't hurt my horse!" Chemita yelled, dropping the lead rope to seize the 30-30 by the barrel.

The rifle lurched in Lucio's hand with a deafening crack. A finger sized blue-black hole appeared almost simultaneously on Chemita's checkered shirt. Chemita let out a shrill, "Ay," just before his startled eyes slowly closed and he crumbled to the ground. Lucio's lunch landed with a clang at the end of Chemita's limp arm causing tamales to tumble out and mix with the stream of blood that was now running from under Chemita.

Lucio dropped to his knees next to where Chemita lay motionless and pleaded with the boy, "Chemita. Alevantate. It was an accident. Deveras."

The sun hung just over the treetops causing the shadows of the tombstones to slither over the mourners gathered around the hole that would be Chemita's final resting place. Julio stood solemnly with a tray of gorditas hoisted up to his chin, silently offering them to those in attendance while Inez poured the chocolate. The mourners accepted the offerings with lugubrious sighs of "such a tragedy" and "que desgracia, killed by his own uncle." Julio overheard some men talking about how they had to take Lucio to be cured of susto because he kept begging to be taken to his tio the matador para que lo matara. Julio was wondering about which uncle Lucio was talking about and if matadors killed people too when the congregation suddenly parted and the women in attendance let out a collective moan that subsided in stuttered wails as Chemita's open coffin was presented for final viewing before burial. Those standing nearest the casket ceased their lament to take note of the blood dripping from the base of the coffin and started casting menacing glares at the village carpenter, who held up his watch in his own defense and mouthed, "No habia tiempo," to the crowd. Hortencia fell silent and focused on the sound of the drops of blood splashing over the broken earth then frantically clutched her ears and wailed, "se me ha muerto el gusto," throwing herself onto the casket, knocking it off the wooden saw horses that were sustaining it. At the sight of this, Quina and a few other women let out cries of their own and began to swoon, provoking their stone-faced husbands to steady them. Once the women were calmed by splashing their faces with rubbing alcohol and the casket righted on the saw horses, the priest began the sermon. Julio balanced the tray he was carrying on a neighboring headstone and made his way through the crowd to the casket and looked inside. Julio saw his cousin's head tilted in death, frail arms crossed gently at the wrist, dainty child hands resting on embroidered ridges running over the breast pockets of a sky blue guayabera doused in crimson. Julio followed the bone-colored buttons to the pleated slacks ironed as sharp as razors all the way down to where the cuffs yielded to expose his cousin's calloused bare feet. They bury you like a pendejo, in a new suit and barefoot, Julio realized. Julio allowed himself to look into his primo's expressionless face, as the steady drone of the priest's sermon merged with the wails from the crowd and the incessant sound of the dripping blood from the coffin, and felt ashamed that he couldn't stop his thoughts from returning to the red stain that was spreading all over his new suit. Julio stood there staring down into the casket watching the stain encroach over his new guayabera. He stood there for a long time.

Eight or perhaps ten years later, Julio crossed the dance floor of the cantina heel to toe with his arm locked around the waist of a woman much taller than him. When the couple reached the end of the bar, Julio plopped down on a barstool and whirled the woman around drawing her to him as he buried his face into her chest. He let his finely trimmed mustache whisk over one breast then the other. The woman braced herself on his strong shoulders arching her back as she pushed the eager young man out of her cleavage and said, "Que mañoso eres muchacho."

"That's a trick my brother Inez taught me." Julio fished in the pocket of his sandstone colored conjunto and drew a fifty-peso coin that he slapped down on the bar and said, "tell me you don't like it so I can find me another dance partner."

The woman remained standing close to him eyeing the coin then began fingering the gold embroidery over the breast pockets of Julio's suit. "I just said you were tricky, not that I didn't like it." She ran her hands up over Julio's chest and laced her fingers through his dark brown locks and pulled his head towards her swaying her shoulders so that he could dedicate equal attention to either breast.

"Why don't you buy us a drink?" she asked after pushing him away again.

"Why don't I buy us a lot of drinks?"

"Just make sure you save some money for later."

Julio let out a grito. "Such a tender girl you turned out to be."

"I was just saying so you know, we could spend more time together."

Julio reached for the coin on the bar and began wrapping the counter with it, "cantinero, bring me something to forget the love I once had for this lady."

The woman giggled then turned Julio's face back into her dress's plunging neckline. The barkeep approached the couple and began wiping down the counter. "You ready for a tequila Julio or are you going to smooth out your mustache some more?"

"I plan on smoothing out a few things before the night is over," Julio said, slapping the woman's rump. "That's for thinking I would choose alcohol over you."

The barkeep poured Julio a double shot of tequila, "Can I get your friend anything?"

Julio slid the fifty-peso coin across the counter and said, "Get her one of those orange juices you pass off as liquor and tell me when this runs out."

The cantinero took the coin then returned with a sherry glass filled with orange juice that he placed in front of the woman perched on Julio's knee. The barkeep reached under the counter and produced a poker chip that he handed to the woman who palmed it and turned so she could stuff the chip in her bra.

"I don't even want to know how many fichas you collect in one night mamita." Julio winked to the barkeep and said, "I bet she makes more than you."

The barkeep waited for Julio to down his tequila then began refilling the glass, "This one's on me," he said.

"Oh?"

"I don't want to spoil your good time or anything, but maybe you can help me with something."

"I'm starting to believe this is going to be the most expensive shot of the night."

"It's nothing really." The cantinero capped the bottle and pointed to a corner table where Lucio Carrillo sat with his back to the wall, a half empty bottle of mescal separating him from the husky man sitting opposite him. "It's just that your uncle Lucio has been drinking all day with don Emilio."

"Isn't that what people do in cantinas?"

"Well yeah, but Lucio's been promising to cut Emilio a deal on some goats. Emilio's been buying bottle after bottle and your uncle hasn't budged a peso."

"Well, he shares the same affection I have for this one here with them goats," Julio said giving the woman a peck on her neck. "He probably wants to charge Emilio for the sentimental value."

"If you could just—"

Julio downed the shot of tequila and slammed the glass down on the counter in front of the barkeep, "Put that on my tab and bring my friend here another fake drink and don't forget to give her her ficha."

The barkeep studied Julio's clenched jaw for a moment then refilled the glass and left to fetch the woman her drink.

The woman stood between Julio's open knees sliding her hands over his shoulders, running her fingers tenderly over the bone-colored buttons centered on the breast pockets. "You're a sharp dresser," she said. "I like sharp dressers."

"Mamacita, how'd you like to take me somewhere I can hang my new suit before you wrinkle it up?" Julio collected his change from the barkeeper and started to make his way across the dance floor with his arm wrapped around the woman's waist. The cantina buzzed with drunken chatter accented with whooping gritos and coquettish giggles until the sound of a crashing table silenced everyone but the jukebox. Julio turned to see his uncle Lucio draw a .32 caliber revolver and shout, "Go ahead and try it, you won't be the first one I've sent to another world."

Lucio's words hit Julio like a thousand bee stings flooding his senses with rage. He didn't see Emilio leveling a .22 at his uncle. He didn't even hear himself scream out his uncle's name. All he could do was focus on the distorted image of his uncle's face turning to see who was rushing at him from the dance floor. Emilio took advantage of the distraction to squeeze off three rounds into Lucio's torso a split second before Julio was able to fill the gap between the two combatants. Lucio teetered and said "Ay sobrino," then collapsed in Julio's arms. Julio staggered a half step back under the weight of his uncle's limp body then let Lucio slide to the floor. Some men were overpowering Emilio, wrestling the gun from his raised hand as Emilio yelled, "He drew first, he drew first."

Julio examined the body lying at his feet and stepped gingerly away to avoid the spreading pool of blood. Julio could hear voices behind him murmuring that he was a brave man to try and step in front of a bullet meant for his uncle. Julio made his way through the gawking crowd to where the woman was standing wide-eyed clutching her cheeks and tried to collect her in his arms but she pushed him away. "No, you'll stain my dress," she protested.

Julio let his hands slide over his chest and stomach. He felt the sticky moistness of his uncle's blood seeping through to his own copper skin. He pulled at his shirt from the waistline and stretched it as far as he could in front of him. He stood there staring at the crimson stain covering his new suit. He stood there like that for a long time.

Pa'l Otro Lado

Rafita's teeth were coming in and there was no money to buy him the medicine that would numb his gums. The teething had gotten so bad that the babe refused to take his mom's breast, causing her to swell and run fever. Ama Quina had tried everything she knew. Cold wraps for her and onion stalks and every tea she could get her hands on, eucalyptus, manzanilla, te de tila for the baby. She even rubbed tequila on Rafita's gums. But he kept crying, louder and louder, with ear splitting shrieks, day after day.

The noise drove Julio mad. The sound of the wailing child was like an invisible hand that backhanded him across the mouth and prevented him from entering the jacal every time he came back from the fields. He took to eating his meals out by the corrals, but sound carries on dusty farms in northern Mexico. Drowsy sobs interrupted by gasping hiccups followed Julio to the river when he took his bath in the evenings and mingled with his own reflection on the swirling white water that rushed between his legs and distorted his features in ways that more accurately portrayed his feelings than his actual features. Worst of all he knew that when his little brother got over the swollen gums, it would be something else another one of his siblings would need. Inevitably one or the other would be bitten by a spider or snake, or thrown or kicked. They'd get sick. The fields wouldn't get enough rain. There'd be nothing for the goats to forage. Coyotes or the train would thin the flock. And every day there had to be something to fill the wailing mouths that resided with him in el jacal grande. For however hard he tried, he could not come up with a solution to any of these problems with what he had at hand.

His father and older brother had been gone six months, having left just after the killing with barely a sparing message that they'd made it pa'l otro lado safely and were in a town called Weslaco just north of the river. The reasoning was that the less the family knew about Cheto's location the better in case some members of the offended family came looking for revenge. But that information was enough in Julio's mind. He had a direction and the name of a town. He figured if he could just keep the town of Los Ramones behind him, he couldn't miss el norte.

He told his mother of his plans to join his father and brother in America. He said that Chetito was old enough to handle all the daily chores. He promised that as soon as he met up with his father, he would make his Apa send her money so she could buy the medicine for Rafita's swollen gums. And he himself would send all he made as soon as he started working. Ama Quina looked at her second born through tear-soaked eyes and said, "What can I tell you? You're already well past twelve. You're old enough to do what you want."

Julio set out to the other side of the Bravo by the light of a full moon carrying four bean tacos, a small jug of water, and his best shirt. Barely being able to keep his pace down to a steady trot, he crossed maize fields and passed the cemetery and then up through the plaza and out of town, arriving at the crossroad to the main highway before the break of day. He waited for the first sparks of daylight and assured himself that he needed to take a left and then headed north with the wind on his back. There was still dew on the brush when he skirted the Rancheria called El Refugio. His legs were not sore at all, but his mouth was dry, and he was out of water. He knew that sooner than later he'd have to drink from the cattle troughs that he passed.

He stood directly under the noon day sun as he read the road marker that announced the town of Los Herreras five kilometers to the left and it was there that he realized that this was the farthest he had ever been from home. He looked around carefully. He studied the farmhouses that rested far from the roadside. He took in the pens and corrals and looked past all of that to the open monte. He saw the twisted mesquite standing alongside the leafy huisache and the thorns and prickly brush that grew on and around the nopales. It was all just as he had imagined. Kilometer after kilometer of uninteresting things. Uninteresting things covered in dust. The road was no different than anything else he had experienced in his short life. The world was as interesting as a passing truck or a man drawing his last breath. He had seen many trucks and only one man draw his last breath and knew that one was just as common as the other. Even as he stood next to Santana and listened to the man who his father just shot choke on his own blood, he knew that there'd be no angels descending from the heavens to carry the soul away. It did not surprise him, but Julio was disappointed to learn that men die the same as the goats and sheep they slaughtered on the Hacienda. Julio could find no more interest than that in the incident. The road he faced stretched before him as plain as the fact that he would get nowhere just standing there thinking.

He trudged north for three days and two nights through town and village, through field and brush, sleeping where he could and always choking on dust and desperate hope every step of the way till a broad river with swirling greenish water flowed at his feet.

He stumbled dizzily along the riverside, half-starved and exhausted looking for a ford to cross. He ran into a group of men who were busy building a campfire and had to change his course a little so as not to walk too close to their camp. One of the men called out to him, "¿A donde vas?"

"Pa'l otro lado."

"Echale chingasos."

The encouragement from a fellow traveler renewed his strength. He looked at the northern bank of the river and the swirling waters between him and decided that further delay was unfathomable. He stripped his clothes and tied them in a bundle with his belt—which was made of rope anyway—and he strapped the bundle to the top of his head. He stood naked on the bank staring down at his reflection. His arms and face were dark and worn, but the rest of his body was as white as the cotton balls that hung from dried limbs in the fields that stretched out north from the river. He could count his own ribs, and his legs looked so thin and knobby that he was amazed they could carry him this far. He took a long look at his face. He had a small but bulbous nose that sat squarely between razor sharp cheekbones. His face was outlined by a rail thin jaw that somehow melded into a stern chin, and there was a hint of a fuzzy shadow growing over his lip. He liked his face, especially his shiny black eyes because they conveyed the readiness he always felt.

"Listo," he said and entered the river.

He waded out till the round slippery rocks below his feet disappeared, and then he let the current take him downstream.

He had already eyed a spot some fifty meters down where he could make his landing. He gently stroked the waters as they carried him moving diagonally to the northern bank. Midway, he turned on his back for a bit to enjoy the view of the crystal blue sky dancing over him. He leaned back and gazed at the immensity of the heavens above him that covered the US and his México querido and stretched even further to the Hacienda and beyond to lands he had never even heard of and laughed because he knew that all who looked to the heavens were just as screwed as him.

In that moment of brief illumination, he felt the current pick up, and he began to spin. The sky that had but a moment ago let itself be opened and seen in all its sincerity now spun and dipped and dived as fiercely as the thrashing currents that now had him in their grip. Julio panicked and started to scream, but his mouth was immediately silenced with an invasion of water. The fluid pushed its way down his windpipe causing him to gag, but also to remember. He willed himself to calmness. He gathered his wits. He had grown up on the banks of a river. Every bath of his life had been taken in that river. This river could not be that different. He thought hard. He was in a whirlpool. He desperately needed to extend his limbs so that the current would push him out instead of dragging him down. He managed to stretch himself out spread eagle and was able to get atop the whirlpool. The sky above him stopped dipping and diving but continued to swirl angrily as he spun head over heel in the green waters of the Bravo. He did not dare to draw another breath for fear of taking in more water and soon found his head light and dizzy. He thought of the many ways he could meet his end and decided that to be found snared and water bloated on some broken branch with onlookers shaking their heads and lamenting, "And he was so close," was one of the worse ways to go, so he thrust his hand out one last time in a final act of defiance and was able to grab hold of some Johnson grass that was growing on the bank. He clung to this weed, even though it was but a small tuft, and managed to pull himself to safety. He lay naked on the northern bank of the Rio Grande, taking in heaving gulps of air and feeling more respect for weeds than he had ever felt in his life.

When he had composed himself, he started down river in search of his clothes that had been ripped off his head in the whirlpool. He walked, naked and ashamed. He found a boot and a sneaker that did not belong to him but that he was able to use just the same. In a clump of cattails, he found his pants but not his shirt or anyone else's. He started up the bank as a plume of dust came rolling toward him. A white truck came at the point of the plume and was engulfed in dirt when it came to a halt in front of Julio. He covered his nose and mouth with his elbow and squeezed his eyes shut to protect himself from the stinging dust that assaulted his bare torso. When Julio felt it safe to open his eyes, he saw he was caked in dirt. The white man sitting on the passenger's side of the pick-up rolled down the window and said, "What?"

Julio mulled the word over in his mind studying the man's expression and somehow knew that an answer was required of him, so he simply said, "Weslaco."

The man in the truck turned to the driver and said, "I'm telling you, Charlie. These fucking wetbacks got it all figured out. They send their nits up here knowing that all we can do is put the little brats up at the juvenile boarding school in Weslaco. Three hots and a cot, and they get to go to school. On our dime." The man opened the door and exited the truck. He took off his straw Texan hat and swatted Julio across his bare shoulder, sending up a little puff of dust and said, "C'mon." The man led Julio to the opening of the caged bed of the truck and then pushed him in. Julio had to squat like a monkey as the truck bounced its way over the rutted roads that surrounded the cotton fields. After a long time and many falls, the truck hit a paved road and shortly after came to a screeching halt that sent Julio tumbling. They were in front of a square building surrounded by a nine-foot chain-link fence with barbed wire looped around the upper edge. There was a sign in front of the building with words that Julio did not understand. But beneath those words, he could read clear as day, *Weslaco, TX*.

They fed him a bowl of oatmeal, a slice of buttered toast, and a glass of orange juice every morning. After breakfast, he was sent to a school room where a thin man wearing glasses and a short-sleeved shirt sat at the front of the room encouraging the class to repeat after him, "*Oh where have you been, Billy Boy, Billy Boy? Oh, where have you been, charming Billy?*" Julio repeated the words as instructed but was confused. He asked another boy, who as it turns out was from General Bravo—a town Julio had passed on his trip north—why they had to know about this boy, Billy? His classmate answered that they were being taught English.

Julio thought about this and realized that it was not English that they were being taught. He did not know what it was, but it wasn't English. He had studied the men who ran the place where they had him and decided that these men spoke an English entirely different than what they were learning in class—not once did he hear these men inquire about *Billy Boy*. He chose to go along with the lessons, or at least act like he was, so he wouldn't be hit with the paddle that the short-sleeved man wielded so willingly. But he was really concentrating on what the men said when they talked amongst themselves and how they spoke to him and the other children when they weren't in class.

In a short time, Julio figured out that in English, every conversation started with the word, "What." It varied in degree of intensity, but "What" and repeating this word a lot seemed to be the means to advance or disrupt many things. He also discovered that there are a lot of words in the English language but only a few are important. He saw how "Goddammit" was frequently used to move people into action. "Oh, hell no," was a polite way to decline or deny anything. And that, "Get the hell out of here," was a favored way of ending conversations and that this last phrase was often emphasized with the throwing of a pencil or whatever else the speaker may be holding at the time. He learned how to be nice in English. Every day after he cleaned the kitchen and was allowed to eat his mid-day meal, the man who was in charge of the cafeteria where they all ate shook his hand and said, "No free lunch, boy," with a big grin that made the tasteless food Julio was given a little easier to swallow. The man always roared with laughter when Julio repeated, "No free lunch."

Julio stayed at this school for six weeks. After the initial shock of having to be in this place wore off, Julio began to grow restless and fretted that he had not caught up to his father and brother yet. He knew that his mother must be insane with worry over how to feed his brothers and sisters, and then there was little Rafita who was probably still crying. He made his mind up that he would leave the first chance he got, and it turned out that freedom was just behind a door in the kitchen.

One afternoon when he was scrubbing pots, the woman cook opened a door in the kitchen and motioned for him to take out a bucket of grease over by the trash cans—she spoke Spanish but had explained how the white men didn't like for the Mexicans to speak Spanish because they felt that they were talking about them. When Julio went outside, he noticed a road running behind the school. Beyond the road were green fields, and he could see men huddled over plants picking cotton. Julio dropped the grease bucket and squeezed himself through the chained gates and trotted over to the men working in the fields.

"Do any of you men know Aniceto Cortina?" Julio asked.

A tall thin man unfolded his body from over a cotton plant and said, "Don Cheto and his son are working over there by the tractor. Make sure you don't bend any of the plants on your way there."

Julio made his way over to the tractor that was hitched to a load of cotton and behind it found his father and brother resting in the shade of the machine. "Hola, Papa," Julio said.

His father shaded his eyes and looked up at his son and said, "Oh, you're here."

"I came because Rafita was crying. He needs medicine."

"Babies always cry. You should've stayed with your mother. The only thing I asked of you was to take care of things while I was away."

"But I had to find you."

"As soon as I turned my back, you run off. Well, gracias. I needed more things to worry about. I left you hundreds of goats and dozens of chickens. What could you lack?"

Now second guessing his choice and desperate to please, Julio offered up his only possession: his back. "I can help you work. I'll pick more than all these guys."

"The work's all but done here. We're waiting to fill this load and then we're going to see el señor Brand to settle on a price to pick his onions."

"I can help with that. I can pick onions."

"Yes, of course, anyone can. And you will, so we can buy you a bus ticket back. But for now, we have to wait for the

Pocho to get here so he can translate for us." The men of the work camp relied heavily on anyone who could speak English and Spanish, even if their skills were limited to Spanglish, so the workers could get a set wage before the labor started. If they did not set a wage at the onset, the grower would stiff them or pay only a fraction of what the work was worth. The negotiations of a bilingual Chicano represented the closest thing to a contract that they could aspire to.

"You don't need a Pocho. I can speak English," Julio said flushed with newfound delight.

"You, speak English," his brother Inez said from under his hat. "Since when?" The words stung Julio. He was still sore that Inez had been chosen to go north instead of him, and to see him like usual on his back napping when all the others were working only confirmed to Julio that he would've been the better choice.

"Oh, yeah. Yes it is, forget it," Julio said in English as coolly as he could. "I studied English for six weeks at that school," He said, pointing to the building he had just escaped in the distance. "I learned a lot. You'll see."

Before Julio could continue his pitch, his father was on his feet and shouting for the others to gather, "Hey, bring the jeep. Mi'jo has been to the gringo school and knows English. He'll get us a good deal with Brand."

A topless Willies Jeep, still painted army green, came bouncing over the rows and to a stop in front of Julio and his father. Don Aniceto scurried around to the driver's side and relieved a man of the keys and climbed in behind the wheel. Julio started for the front seat but was pulled back by his older brother. "The kids ride in the back. The men ride in the front."

Julio reluctantly crawled between the seats and sat in the back of the jeep. A half dozen men piled into the jeep next to Julio, their legs dangling haphazardly next to the grinding back wheels. They drove to a small store made of bare cider blocks where other men sat lazily under the shade of twisted mesquite trees drinking out of containers they concealed in brown paper bags. Julio's father came out of the little store with a fudge popsicle that he gave to his son. He had had popsicles before but those were made of aguas frescas of lemon and melon, but this treat that his father had bought him was ice cream on a stick, and it was amazing.

"Now, Julio, I want you to speak your best English and get us a good deal," Don Cheto said, bending down so he could look his son in the eye. Julio nodded excitedly and tried hard to lick up the popsicle to keep the melted chocolate goodness from running over his fingers and down his chin, but not with much luck. "Pay attention now," His father said, shaking a two-gallon pail in front of his son. "We want twenty cents a pail, vez? But you have to ask for more so he'll come down to twenty, you get it?"

Julio kept devouring the popsicle but made it known that he was ready. His father handed him a bandana to clean his hands and face then walked him over to a tall man in a white shirt and red cap with the words "Griffon Brand Inc." stitched over the visor.

Don Cheto stood between his son and Mr. Brand and said, "Meester Brand, mí Julio." Julio saw that he was going to have to deliver on his promise and began to worry. Julio stood there with his hands dangling at his side, the fudge popsicle dripping its cool delights to the dirt, until finally he mustered up his nerve and with great conviction said, "What?"

Brand said, "Well, I need all the men you got and I'm willin' to pay top dollar, fifteen cents a pail."

Julio, seeing that it was his turn to speak again, repeated as loud as he could, "What?"

"Fifteen cents is good money, boy. You shore aint gonna git any better 'round here," Brand said, first looking at the sliver of a child before him then to the other men standing around who were now on their feet encircling the pair. Brand could see that the same men who but moments ago were deeply invested in showing the greatest indifference were now becoming menacingly interested in their conversation. When he turned his gaze back to Julio, the boy realized that it was time to show his English. He raked his brain and found the words that he learned at the school: "Oh, goddamit." The befuddled look that came over Brand caused Julio to worry that he had not spoken the right words, but he remembered that he had not made the right face or done the right actions, so he repeated, "Oh, goddammit." And then threw what remained of the popsicle to one side making sure to look disgusted while doing it. Julio was scared and thrilled all at once but was not even sure how the dealing was going. He had learned about English numbers but he only knew how to use them to count "little Indian boys." He threw every word in his arsenal at the white man towering over him, "Oh, damn shit hell. Git the hell outa here." He realized that he had nothing to throw, so he kicked the pail and balled his fists and clenched his body, forcing all the blood to his face in the hopes that a vein would swell on his forehead like it did on the man with glasses at the school. The look that came across Julio's face upset the other men, so they grunted and balled their fists too.

Brand looked taken aback, and Julio figured that his English must be better than even he thought it to be because Brand responded in terms Julio could understand.

"Goddammit, I'll go twenty cents but you greasers better have this field clean in three days," Brand said, taking off his red cap and waving it at the field of onions that stretched out to the horizon behind him. The men crowded even closer and shuffled and elbowed each other waiting for the boy to close the deal.

Brand stood before the boy with mouth agape. "Well I'll be hanged. A goddamn Mexican that doesn't come a beggin'." Looming over Julio, Brand's lips curled into a grin. He picked up the pail the boy had kicked his way and hurled it hard over the group's heads. He stuck out his hand to Julio and said, "Twenty cents a *bucket* and not a penny more, you sewer-mouthed wetback sonofabitch."

Julio took Brand's hand and said grinning, "No free lunch."

Brand tossed the boy's hand and turned to Julio's father and said, "Take care of this one. He's uppity enough to grow up to be somethin' in this world if somebody doesn't shoot him first." Brand stepped into his white Ford sedan and yelled from the open window, "Now yawl better be here by sun-up, or I'm finding some other wets."

The men fell in around Julio and the next thing he knew he was being carried high over everyone's head. His father was getting pats on the back and even his big brother Inez was smiling in delight. Don Cheto scurried over to the Jeep and said, "C'mon mi'jo. Let's get something to eat."

"I want another one of those paletas," Julio said matter-of-factly.

"Sure, mi'jo. I want to get something anyway," Cheto said hurrying back into the store to get his son another nieve. Inez grabbed Julio by the arm and tried lifting him to the back of the Jeep but Julio resisted. Their father returned with the popsicle and some meat wrapped in butcher paper and ordered his sons into the Jeep. Don Cheto started the machine with the boys still not in the Jeep. "Chingada Madre, Inez. Get in. It's late. I'm hungry, and tonight we can afford to eat like people."

Julio took the seat next to his father's and started to unwrap the popsicle but stopped when he caught sight of his brother's grimacing face through the rearview mirror. Julio handed back the popsicle to his brother and watched him hurriedly unwrap it and shove half of it in his mouth before they could even take the road.

Julio smiled and settled himself into his seat and said, "You have the paleta, Inez. Those things are for kids anyway." The men who were crammed next to his big brother laughed and tousled Julio's hair.

The following morning Julio was still dozing when the jeep pulled up to Brand's field. A group of men were huddled around stacks of buckets that were twice as big as the pails they had been used to filling. Julio was still trying to figure out what the problem was when he felt a stinging blow to the back of his head. His ears rang and his eyes bulged from the slap. His father stood over him ready to land another before saying, "Maybe someday you'll be good for something like the man said, but today isn't it." The second blow whacked him on the side of the head and sent him tumbling over the stacked buckets. He lay on his back befuddled. The men looking down at him laughed. His brother Inez laughed the loudest.

La Olla

Virginia Perez was fifteen when Jose Maria Cortina rode up to her and asked, "Are you going to marry my son or not?"

She was shucking corn and only looked up long enough to say, "Cheto said he was going to ask me, but he didn't say when. Then he asked me to meet him behind the corrals. That'll be the day, I told him."

Don Chema snorted and spurred his horse. The next day, Aniceto Cortina rode up to the Perez spread leading a burro laden with a fifty-kilo sack of beans and another of rice. He got off his horse and winced with each creaky step he took in his new patent leather shoes that were a size too small. They were the only pair in the store that came close to fitting him, but his father had told him to look respectable when he went courting, so he bought them even though they hurt his feet. Virginia, or Quina as everyone called her, laughed as he walked up imagining her suitor going headfirst and killing himself before he even made his way into her parlor.

"You must have your toes tucked behind your heels, Cheto," she said as he passed through her front door.

Quina's mother twisted up her mouth and tugged on her daughter's hair while pointing an accusing finger. Quina sucked her teeth and directed her guest into the living room where they had set up chairs and a table for coffee and pan dulce. "Ask Cheto what news he brings from his travels, mi'ja," her mother said through clenched teeth.

"I don't know what news he could have that we haven't heard yet being that we live in the same town," Quina said curtly.

"They found a sheepherder hanging from a mesquite the other day. I wonder what he must of felt just hanging there," Cheto said, taking his seat.

"He was probably upset that you bought the last pair of patent leather shoes in the store," Quina said. Her mother swooned and had to be helped to her seat.

Before Cheto left that night, he handed Quina a ten-peso coin and told her that he'd be supporting her now. They were married a year later.

Cheto was the youngest of the Cortina boys. Quina sized up her sisters-in-law and knew she'd have the whole clan squaring off to her before all was said and done. She kept the cleanest house, had the most children, and was her mother-in-law's favorite. This fact was confirmed when Mama Candida gave her la olla just before she died.

It was a magnificent clay pot. It was bigger than the ones they sold in the plaza and was cured in such a fashion that nothing, no matter how burnt, which she never did, ever stuck or stained that olla.

The clay pot had belonged to Mama Candida from the day Papa Chema went and asked for her hand in marriage. He brought it with him and put it in her hands. It had belonged to Apa Chema's mother, Mama Quirina, and God only knows where that witch got the clay pot. The olla was Quina's now and since it was her husband who had killed that scoundrel who tried to kill her father-in-law, Quina was the woman who everyone had to toe the line for, and the role fit her. She could cook the best meals. She could raise the healthiest children. She knew what to do when someone was sick. She knew what to say when someone tried to get out of line. And she knew that no matter what, she could say any goddamn thing that came to her mind, and everyone had to take it.

For eighteen months, while her father-in-law was in jail and her husband hiding from the law in Texas, Quina ran everything. Apa Chema had taken the blame for the killing of Santana even though everyone knew it was Quina's husband Cheto who had shot Santana off his horse. Cheto also put a bullet in Santana's brother Facundo when the sneaky bastard tried to pick up Santana's gun and shoot Cheto. She drove the cart that took Santana and the wounded Facundo back to their spread and when their sisters tried to keep their mother from seeing her dead son and blaming her for being mistress to Apa Chema, it was Quina who hopped off the cart and confronted the daughters face to face.

"Es tu madre. Es la madre de tu hermano. Ustedes no son nadie para juzgar."

But the girls did judge their mother and they judged Apa Chema. Now that their brothers were dead, Facundo lingering for months then dying from the hole in his kidney, the three sisters gathered and discussed the situation. They sold livestock and pooled their money and then headed for Laredo. It was in Laredo that they found the man. For ten thousand pesos he agreed to kill Jose Maria Cortina.

As soon as Apa Chema was released from jail—he was exonerated on the grounds of self-defense—he headed to the cantina. He was drinking tequila with beer chasers when the assassin sauntered into the cantina and made his way down the bar to where Apa Chema stood pounding shots and cheering the mariachi with woops and gritos.

"Mister, I don't know you but I'm willing to bet you won't sell this bender for all the money in the world," the man said, holding his finger up to order a shot for himself.

"You got that one right, young man," Chema said gleefully. "I have plenty to celebrate. I just spent 18 months in hell and now I'm free and soon my boy can come home. Nothing could make me give up these bottles of tequila that have embraced my joy and refused to let go."

"I like your style, mister," the man said. "I like your manner. It reminds me of me. We even wear the same type of gun."

Apa Chema palmed the grips of his .32 Smith and Wesson and eyed the man standing next to him at the bar. "You handy with that gun, señor?"

"There's only one way to find out. Let's go outside and find something to shoot at," the killer said as he walked to the door.

Apa Chema followed him out and both men impressed the crowd that had spilled out of the cantina with fancy pistol work. Chema shot three bottles off a fence post then turned and said, "Now you."

The stranger pulled his gun and spent six shots knocking off two prickly pears off a cactus. Apa Chema examined the man's shooting and determined that he was a novice at best.

"You need a little practice, young man," Chema said. "Don't worry. You'll get better with time."

"I won't get much practice with an empty gun," the killer said with a grin.

Chema Cortina emptied his gun and handed the bullets over to his assassin. "There's only three unspent, but half a load is better than none."

The stranger took the cartridges in his palm and looked hard at them. "But now your gun is empty."

Apa Chema kicked a clump of dirt and snapped his fingers for someone to bring him another drink, which they did. And he drank straight from the bottle before offering it to the man, saying, "I'm from here. My spread is just down the road. I got plenty of ammunition at home."

"But your gun is empty now," he said.

"That doesn't concern me," Apa Chema said. "What kind of man doesn't help a stranger when he can?"

The killer loaded the three bullets into his own gun and leveled it at Apa Chema, "The kind of man who gets paid to kill assassins." The coward emptied the three bullets into Apa Chema and ran away.

Chema fell holding his ribs. He pulled himself up to his knees but the men from the cantina forced him to lie down and they sent for a car. They loaded him up in a new Ford Model-A and sped off at 35 kilometers per hour to Monterrey to get Don Chema to a doctor.

Quina was knee deep in the Pesqueria river washing her olla when she saw the group of women descend the banks. She gathered her skirt and gave her olla a final dunk and rinsing. The splashing water had soaked her dress, but Quina couldn't see the bump of a baby yet, but she knew it was there just the same. She knew her own body and she had felt the stirrings of life from the moment of conception the night Cheto had sneaked back into town. She was almost out of the river with her olla hoisted on her hip when the group of women wailed and blurted out the news that her father-in-law had been shot and feared dead. Her knees buckled and the whole world started to spin. She felt her olla leave her hands and heard it shatter on a clump of rocks. She thought she might have seen the broken pieces floating in the swift current, but she couldn't be sure because at that very moment everything went black.

Quina woke up to a room full of people. Her children, Chetito and Rafita, were crying at the foot of her bed. Someone had lined chairs against her walls and in each chair sat a woman praying the rosary. Quina looked around the room and was about to ask what the hell was going on when she noticed the smell. She picked up a piece of her night-gown—someone had changed her—and took a deep whiff.

"Why do I smell like piss?" Quina demanded.

La Tia Tencha tried to explain, "We told you about your father-in-law and you fainted."

"I was awake for that part," Quina said, kicking the covers off her and sitting up in a blood-stained bed. "Why do I have pee all over me?"

It was one of the ladies from El Refugio, Doña Carmela, who told her. "We bathed you in our pee so you wouldn't go into shock."

"Who the hell told you that bathing someone in pee was good for not going into shock?" Quina yelled at the room. "Get me a bucket of water and some clean sheets. Get me something for me to wear. See if you can at least do that right, you bunch of cochinas. Can't you see I just lost a baby?"

"What are you going to do?" Tia Tencha asked while pulling a clean dress out of the armoire.

"I'm going to go see what happened to my father-in-law," Quina said.

Quina went by the cemetery and made Fidencio ride in her cart with her to Monterrey. "It doesn't look right for a woman to travel alone," she said.

It was nearly four in the morning when she got to the hospital. She had no trouble finding her father-in-law's room. All she had to do was follow the Mariachi music. Her father-in-law was drawing his last breath when Quina came into the room. She waited for the last notes of *Que Viva Mi*

Desgracia to finish and then went and sat on the edge of the bed and took the dying man's hand in hers.

"¿Que te paso?" Her eyes welled with tears.

Chema looked up and smiled, "I trusted a man."

She was going to tell him that trusting a man is the stupidest thing a person could do but it was too late. Jose Maria Cortina was dead.

Quina ran her palm over her father-in-law's eyes and made them close. She let her hand linger on his cheek for a moment then turned to the men in the room and asked, "where's his gold watch?"

The Mariachi exited and the remaining men held up their palms and stared off into space. Quina sucked her teeth and ordered the remains of her father-in-law to be loaded up into her cart. She left right after settling the bill at the hospital.

The sun was going down again when she rode into her patio. Her boys ran out and started to cry when they saw the lifeless body of their grandfather lying in their cart. Quina stopped them by ordering them to help her lift the body out and into her bed.

"We'll pray for him tonight and bury him tomorrow," she told the boys.

She had just gotten the body into bed and combed his hair when the people from town arrived. She picked up her rosary and stood at her door to receive the mourners. Men came running up to her and one of them exclaimed, "They have Don Chema's killer trapped in the schoolhouse. Hurry and prepare the gun for Chetito so he can go kill him." Chetito bolted back into his mother's house to retrieve his grandfather's gun.

"Chetito is just a boy. Wait till Julio gets home. He'll kill that motherless coward. I've sent word to el otro lado. Cheto and the boys will be back soon."

"It will be too late," the men pleaded. "The police are going to arrest the killer."

"Then Julio will kill him some other day," Quina said as she went back into the house.

By the time her husband and two eldest sons made it home, Quina had all of the pistols and rifles loaded and ready. "They have him down at the jail," she said as she handed her husband a gun.

She took Julio to one side and held him by the shoulders and bent down to look him in the eye. "They have the jail surrounded waiting for you and your father to try and kill the assassin. Don't try anything tonight. You'll only end up killing the officers."

Quina squeezed her son's shoulders hard and said, "All you have to do tonight is get a good look at him. Take a good look and never forget his face. The day will come and then you can avenge your blood."

Julio made his way around the jail while his father spoke with the officers. He had his brother Inez lift him till he could reach the bars covering the window. He pulled himself and peered through the bars. The man was standing with his back to him but he got a good look. He let the image burn in his heart before saying, "Turn around and look at who is going to kill you." But the man did not turn around even though it was clear that he heard Julio's words. Julio held onto the bars for as long as he could then slipped back to the ground and joined his father and brother.

Cheto took his sons home and approached his wife who was sitting next to his dead father. "Half the town is siding with me and the other half is siding with Santana's family."

"Did the police tell you this?" Quina asked.

"Yes, and everyone else that I ran into on the road. We're going to have a hell of a fight," Cheto said. "Where's Chetito?"

"He's out with his cousin Rueben by the corral. I knew this feud would come to this."

The stillness of the night exploded with gunfire. Quina threw her back against a wall and watched her husband pull his gun before saying, "They're not shooting toward us. It came from the corral."

Cheto was bent over poking the curtain open with the barrel of his gun. He straightened up and opened the door. Chetito and Rueben came running in holding up their palms.

"There were men sneaking up from behind the house and we opened up on them with abuelito's gun," Chetito said.

"We went to where they were and look, this was all over the ground," Rueben said.

The boys stood in the middle of the room holding up their palms, proud to show everyone the blood on their hands.

Right after they buried Apa Chema, Quina made her husband load up the house and move the whole family to the United States. They were traveling out of town in the truck Cheto had brought from el otro lado when she stiffened her back and sat up in her seat. She had forgotten to pack her olla and was about to scold herself for being so careless when she remembered it had broken that day in the river. It seemed like so long ago now. Cheto looked over to his wife and asked her what was wrong.

"Nothing," she said. "I thought we were going to have to go back, but then I remembered that there's nothing to go back for."

They traveled at a steady pace with the truck pointing north at all times.

Dirty Mexicans

Cayetano Perez stood gagging in a cloud of dust made by an angry white man. Cayetano was checking the oil of his Ford when the white man pulled up in an Oldsmobile and ordered Cayetano to "Fill 'er up." Cayetano politely told the white man that he did not work at the gas station and that he was only checking his own oil, and the white man sped off sending up large plumes of dust that stung Cayetano's face and made his nose burn.

When he finished wiping his eyes and spitting out dust, Cayetano slipped behind the wheel of his car. Before he could turn the key, Adela asked, "¿Que es fuck you, Cayetano?"

Cayetano's back stiffened and his face got redder. He put the car in gear and floored the gas hoping to raise as much dust as the white man. "Callete el hosico, vieja sonsa. A lady doesn't use those words."

"Ah-huh, I knew it. That man cussed you," Adela said, folding her arms in front of her and nodding her head. "¿Que es fuck you, Cayetano?" she asked again. "That gringo wanted you to do something, and you told him no and he got mad and said, 'fuck you,' right, Cayetano?" She turned toward her husband and asked, "¿Que es fuck you, Cayetano?"

Cayetano wrestled with the steering wheel concentrating hard on keeping his Ford in its lane. "It's like telling someone que se chinge," he said after some thought.

Adela nodded her head mulling over his words with her arms crossed in front of her. "It's like a mentada de madre, isn't it, Cayetano?" she said with anger.

Cayetano settled himself in his seat and said, "No, not like telling someone to do that to their mother. It's not as bad as that. Only Mexicans are dirty enough to bring their mothers into an insult."

"But it is an insult, right, Cayetano?" Adela said, leaning into her husband's view. "Why didn't you beat that man, Cayetano? You never let any Mexican insult you, Cayetano." She sat back in her seat and watched the road ahead of her. The furrowed fields raced past her window and the hot air blowing through the car scattered her hair across her face. After a few miles, she turned to her husband again and asked, "Was it because he was a gringo, Cayetano? Do you think he knows the patron, Cayetano?"

Cayetano checked his mirrors before answering, "Of course he knows el patron. And the man who rents us our house. And the man who sells us our groceries. All these gringos know each other." Cayetano stuck out his arm and then nosed his car around a truck loaded with melons. "If a Mexican fights with a gringo, there will always be big trouble," he said.

"Yes, the whole world knows that, Cayetano," Adela said, hanging her head. She looked at her shoes and tried scraping the dirt off her heel with the tip of her other shoe but the caked soil only flaked and stained both shoes and left dust on the carpet. "The gringos don't like us because they think they're better than us."

Cayetano glanced down and saw the mess his wife had made on his clean carpet and said, "Maybe the gringos aren't wrong to think that." He turned the car off the asphalt highway and followed a farm road that ran in front of a string of wooden houses sitting on blocks. "We Mexicans are a dirty people. Just look at these houses and their dirty yards. Broken down cars with flat tires. No flowers. No grass. Now look at the gringo's house with the clean yard and the pretty grass." Cayetano shook his head knowingly. "We are a dirty people."

"We don't have clean yards, but look at the fields, each row as straight as a board and not one weed. Not even a clump out of place, acre after acre," she said, filling her chest with air. "We do that. Who has time or strength to clean a yard after so much work? The gringo can do it because he has us to do everything else for him."

Cayetano sucked his teeth. "In Mexico, we worked from sunup to sundown. Every day. Mexicans cross the river and all of the sudden they can only work eight hours and they want to join unions. They think just because they made it here they can stick out their hands and somebody's gonna fill it with money. That's why the gringo doesn't like us."

Adela kept her eyes on the row of houses speeding by her window. "How can the gringo tell just by looking at a person if they are lazy or not?"

Cayetano's mouth fell open. He turned and looked at his wife then back to the road and said, "They don't just look at a person. They know. Doesn't El Henry treat me good?"

Adela shrugged her shoulders.

"You know that he does. He gives me the most hours because he knows I work hard. The gringo is not as dumb as people think," Cayetano said, feeling like he was right.

"Then why do the white ladies cut in front of us at the groceries?" Adela asked, bringing her knees up into the seat to face her husband. "I was there at the butchers with my comadre Lucha about to ask him for a pound of ground, and this white lady came right up and took my turn. I told Lucha loud so the white woman could hear that some people have no manners. I know the gringa didn't understand Spanish, but she knew what I meant. And you know what Lucha did?" Adela sat facing her husband and when he did not reply she shook his arm and asked, "Do you know what my comadre Lucha did? She ran out of the store. Left all her groceries. Oh, and left me talking to myself like a fool. And you know what she said later?"

Cayetano pretended not to care. He wished his wife for once would be quiet. He had the job he had to do on his mind and was sorry he had ever stopped to check the oil. His wife shook his arm again and Cayetano said, "No. No, I don't know what comadre Lucha said later."

Adela could not get her words out fast enough. "She said that I shouldn't say things like that because someone could tell me *something*. I told her that someone should tell that gringa *something*."

Cayetano shook his head and slowed the car down to dodge a couple of potholes. "You shouldn't say things like that," he said. "That's another reason why the gringos don't like us. You try to argue with them in Spanish. The gringo only wants to hear English. Then you have people like my comadre Lucha running out of stores like an Indian," Cayetano scoffed. "And people wonder why the white people don't like them."

"There's no law that says I have to speak English," Adela said.

Cayetano's mouth fell open again, "Hah, no law? No law? This is America. Of course you have to talk in English."

"Yo puedo decir lo que me de mi chingada gana," Adela said, turning to face the road.

Cayetano drove his car over a cattle guard and followed

a mesquite-lined road to the river's edge. He parked the car just as the sun was going down. In the darkness, he told his wife, "They should be already waiting on the other side. If they're not all there, I'm not waiting. I'm coming with whoever's there."

"You'll wait if my sister's not there, won't you Cayetano?" Adela's voice cracked with worry.

"Chingada madre," Cayetano said unbuttoning his shirt. "Only because she's your sister, but you see what I mean? Help a Mexican come to los United and they won't even be on time." He got out of the car and stripped out of the rest of his clothes.

"You're getting paid," Adela said under her breath. Adela followed her husband out of the car and held a plastic bag open for him to place all of his clothes. Adela shook her and said, "Mexicans have to get as naked as the day they were born just to come work for white people."

Cayetano held the bag with his clothes high over his head as he stroked the green waters of the Rio Bravo to Mexico. He had to wait for several hours and was only happy that there was no moon out when he started back to the American side of the river leading four men and Adela's pregnant sister. It was for her that he had to wait. Her belly was big and round and it took her forever to get her clothes off and into the water. He had had to lift her onto an inner tube that he pulled while the other men pushed as they swam across the river to the American side. As he swam, Cayetano warned the group he was guiding, "If we get caught by the migra, remember that we all say we were coming alone. There's no coyote. Understand? We'll get in more trouble if the border patrol thinks there's a coyote in the group." The truth was that only Cayetano would get in more trouble but he was not about to let that secret out. Cayetano did not trust Mexicans.

As soon as the group made it to shore, Adela grabbed her sister and took her into the reeds to get her dressed. The men pulled up the inner tube and began tearing open the plastic bags that held their clothes. There came a crackle of boots on brush and one of the men gasped, "La migra."

Flashlights illuminated the riverbank. Cayetano and the other men stood naked, bathed in the light. "No se mueva, sons of bitches," a voice said from behind a flashlight. A couple of lights turned off and three men dressed in green came forward. The agents snatched the bags with the men's clothing and threw the bundles back into the river. A tall white border patrol agent stepped up to one of the men and said, "Quien es el coyote?" This last word he pronounced Kah-yo-tee. The naked man standing next to the agent stammered, "Venemos solos."

The tall white man dressed in green pulled out a .357 Magnum and drew back on the hammer and then placed the barrel on the naked man's temple and asked again, "Quien es el Kah-yo-tee?"

"Cayetano Perez," the naked man said, pointing to Cayetano.

The tall white man turned his gun on Cayetano and motioned for him to step forward. Cayetano stepped forward and the agents put him in cuffs. Cayetano shook his head and said, "Didn't I tell you that we Mexicans are a dirty people? Come on Adela, they got us."

More flashlights came on and soon two pairs of eyes gleamed from the reeds growing on the edge of the river. Adela and her half naked sister were led out and marched up the bank by the agents. As Adela passed, she turned to her husband and said, "Fuck you, Cayetano."

How They Met

Mary Ann Chavez was the most beautiful woman ever to work in the fields. It's possible that she could have been the most beautiful woman in the world if some Hollywood producer had discovered her. But even in obscurity, Mary Ann, or Anita, which was favored over her given name, was desired by every man who laid eyes on her and envied by every woman she met. There wasn't anything singularly remarkable about her, although you could not find an imperfect feature on her either. On top, firm and perky that could barely fill a man's hand, but more than a few fell face first in the furrowed fields trying to get a peek down her shirt to see but a glimpse of the velvet flesh of her darling breasts. She had a slender waist, curved shapely hips and firm yet not too ample glutes that filled out her denim work pants that zipped on the side like a shell. Anita was not tall, but far from being a flaw, her size was more proof of how extraordinarily attractive she was. It was as if God made her a compact five and half feet tall so that people could take in her whole frame in one breathtaking glance, a sort of gift to mankind like the rainbow the Lord presented to Noah.

It was that, the whole picture, the full image of Anita

that made her so beautiful. From head to toe, she was grace personified. Not one to get too friendly with the other field hands, Anita rarely had conversations with any one person. When she did speak, it was to everyone at once. Her discourse was sharp and pointed and sliced almost painlessly and so effortlessly that the tiny cuts her tongue made were a pleasure to endure and only stunned and ached when she stopped talking.

Her father was the first Mexican-American to own a business in Edinburg. And not just anywhere in Edinburg, Don Alfredo's Mexican Cuisine was located right on the main plaza by the courthouse and the Citrus movie theater. Judges and lawyers ate there. Don Alfredo's did such a thriving business that Anita never lacked any of the finer things a girl could desire--ruffled panties, silky sox, shiny shoes, nice dresses and cute shorts for the summer time. But then, when she was in the middle of her tenth year of grade school—so close to finishing and being able to enter college and then become a doctor—her father ran away with their housekeeper leaving the family penniless. There was work in the fields picking cotton, so Anita and her mother and sisters all got jobs.

She missed her old life, but knew she would somehow get it back. What bothered her were the things that could never be again like playing in the high school band. She missed playing cumbias on her clarinet when Mrs. Winnie left the room. She could never be part of anything like that now, and that hurt her. The past was gone and the present was miserable but the future was still there and she knew it was just time and nothing more. And now just happened to be a bad time; there would be better—although, deep down inside she feared there would not.

Unbeknownst to Anita, but only minutes away, there was

a man. At 18, Julio Cortina could tear down the whole world and build it back up again but didn't out of pity for those who couldn't be as great as him. Last night, he almost broke this rule he made by tearing through the town of Weslaco. It was the dog days of summer and instead of withering in the blazing heat like everyone else, Julio had himself a time. The day started off ordinary enough. The work truck blared its horn at a quarter to five and thanks to an unseasonal heavy dew that morning that made the cotton moist and heavy, Julio had his 400 pounds picked by noon, so he hit the town determined to buy a $1.98 dress shirt south of the tracks in el lado Americano of Weslaco. He strolled down the shaded walk as conspicuously as he could, stopping to look in each window and taking in the displays from as many angles his body could contort.

He was just about to purchase a fine white shirt with light blue pin stripes when Mundo Galvan came up and asked him if he knew anybody who could cross a family from el otro lado.

"How many people we talking 'bout here?"

"Five. Three men and two ladies. One of the men is real old," Mundo said in a hushed voice trying to escape the notice of the gringa sales lady.

"That's going to cost you $35 Americanitos," Julio said coyly.

"Thirty-five dollars?! I'm not asking for you to walk them across the bridge," Mundo protested.

"Yeah, I know. But the current is swift. And I'm going to need some help with the old guy and the ladies, and that's supposing the other two pendejos can swim," Julio said smoothly, knowing that no one could do the job as well as he could do at any price.

Mundo agreed, so Julio instructed him to gather the

group and meet him at the river's edge by the twisted mesquite on the Mexican side.

Julio went and found his older brother Inez and told him of the group that was willing to pay to be brought across.

"How much?" Inez asked greedily.

"Two bucks a head."

"So we both get five bucks each? Well, you've got that all wrong," Inez said matter-of-factly. Before Julio could defend his offer, Inez continued, "I'm getting six dollars and you're getting four because I have the innertubes we'll need to get those people across."

Julio stood with his mouth agape, which only caused Inez to bellow with laughter. "You have to get up mighty early to get the better of your big brother, Julio. Don't you ever forget that."

Julio shrugged and said, "You got me this time. Now, let's get them tubes and get to work."

They put the ladies on a tube each and made their husbands swim alongside during the crossing. Julio laid the old man belly up across an inner tube and guided his cargo gently along with the current. Inez swam ahead and was out of the water before Julio could get the first of the rafts to shore. He had to abandon his charge while he sliced through the water and caught up with the ladies' tubes and got them on to the bank. The old man was frantic when Julio came back for him but otherwise safe. Inez took in the whole scene from the bank clutching his sides and slapping his knees in over dramatized mockery.

It was still an easy trip and Julio got paid well for it. He bought his shirt and had dinner at a place that had napkins made of stiff cloth. Then he hit the cantina from end to end. He did tequila shots with beer chasers at the bar. He snorted cocaine in the bathroom and smoked marijuana behind the building with a bunch of rough customers where the tips of their cigarettes made a scandalous glow with each deep inhale. He ambled home in darkest night and had only closed his eyes for what seemed like an instant when the work truck blared its horn. In his haste not to miss his ride, Julio had to put on his good shoes without any socks. He made it to the back of the truck just as it was pulling away but was able to grab hold of the railing and hoist himself up. He boarded the truck clumsily and headfirst but he managed to steady himself with his body bent at the waist and his face just inches away from Anita's wonderful eyes. He looked into those eyes for only a split second and was asleep as soon as he found a space, but in that brief moment that he held her gaze, Julio was overwhelmed with a sensation that something joyous had just entered his life. In the minutes it took the truck to lumber to the fields, Julio dreamed of an entire life with Anita. Even before his eyelids had betrayed him and were half closed as he was sinking into sleep, he knew it was not that he had to have her, but, and most importantly, that no one else could have her.

When the truck came to a dusty halt at the edge of a field, Julio was the first off, but he made time fidgeting with the two-by-four board the workers hitched to their belts where they fastened their sacks. Anita selected her rows to pick before he entered the field. He had to run off Oscar Lopez but got the rows next to Anita and set himself to ripping the cotton from its bulb at a feverish pace that he made look easy. He was well ahead of Anita when she looked up from the labor with a gasp. Julio was encroaching on her rows and picking her cotton. She had been startled on the truck when his face almost crashed into hers and would have given him an earful had he not looked so embarrassed and asked for pardon all the way to his seat, but to see him steal from her rows was more than infuriating; it was disrespectful. Anita hurried her pace and began to inch her way closer to where Julio had been picking her row, and then she saw the first of what would be many small piles of cotton picked and gathered for her to just stuff in her sack. There was still a vast distance between her and Julio but she was able to gain ground quickly without the burden of actually picking the cotton. She finally caught up with Julio but only because he was waiting for her at the end of the rows.

She stomped up to him and got her face close enough to his to make his grin a little nervous. "Why are you stealing my cotton?" Anita demanded.

"I'm not taking it from you. I'm leaving it there for you so you won't have to bother," Julio said as casually as he could muster.

"Yeah, but how much are you putting into your sack before you make the piles? Huh? It's bad enough that Eusebio robs us at the scales, but now I have to guard my rows from thieving mojaditos," Anita said, throwing up her hands as she spoke.

"I'm not a mojado," Julio protested. He fumbled in his back pocket and pulled out a worn wallet. With hands shaking with fury, he forced out a shiny green card and exposed a small stack of crisp dollars. "You see, I got papers."

"So? People with papers steal too," Anita said, trying hard not to smile. The fact that he had papers, and was not just another undocumented field hand, made her feel good. But not good enough to forget what had started her confrontation. "Look, you pick your rows and let me pick my rows. Then we can all be robbed at the scales."

"Eusebio doesn't take that much. Just a few pounds from each sack so he can get something at the end of the day too," Julio said, trying to get a hold of the meeting. "I don't worry too much about it because I got things going on the side. I do all right for myself." Julio had his chin stuck up so high, he momentarily lost sight of his desire standing right in front of him. He took a half step forward and looked at her hard. "I can do enough for both of us."

"You certainly do for yourself," Anita said, backing away and turning to the fields. "You do for yourself, Eusebio does for himself, and everyone takes my cotton." Anita looked at the row of cotton that laid ahead and felt the sting of the sun that would be in her face for several acres. A knot grew in her stomach. "If I were a man. If I were a man, I wouldn't let Eusebio rob me at the scales. If I were a man, I wouldn't let you nowhere near my rows."

"I don't know why you're so mad," Julio said, catching up to Anita before she could get to work. "I just wanted to get your attention so I could tell you something."

"What?"

Julio stiffened his back and said with all the sincerity he knew, "Me gustas para la madre de mis hijos."

Anita shrieked. "You want me to have your children? I've heard some lines before but yours has to be the craziest."

Julio's face burned with rage. "Who's been talking to you about such things? Eusebio?"

Anita looked at the stern look on Julio's face and the vein on his neck that was pulsating and didn't know whether to laugh or run. She pushed passed him and took to her row.

Julio fell in behind her but was soon well ahead and was still picking Anita's rows and leaving behind piles of cotton. The whole time he kept running their talk through his head looking for signs of interest. He couldn't believe it but he felt doubt that he might've not impressed her. Most girls withered with just a coquettish glance. Why was she different? Why didn't she gush over him? Could there be someone else? She kept talking about Eusebio. Was she interested in him? No, she hated him. She thought he was a thief. Now that he thought about it, Eusebio was a pinche thief. He got a check for working the scales. He was skimming from each sack. Only a few pounds. It seemed too petty a thing to even consider before today. He stopped and looked over his shoulder and gave Anita his most dashing smile, but she just sucked her teeth and picked cotton as fast as she could. He waited for her at the end of the row but she trudged past him with her chin leading the way to the truck where the scales were. She lugged her sack of cotton up to Eusebio who snatched it up and emptied it onto the scale. The brass arm on the scales raced to 56 and came to a bobbing stop on 54. Eusebio announced, "Fifty."

"How many?" Anita asked incredulously.

"You heard," Eusebio said without looking up from his ledger. But the words hardly escaped his lips before Julio was on the truck swinging the two by four that the workers hitched to their belts so they could hang their sacks. The board slapped Eusebio stingingly across the face as Julio let out a guttural, "Cuantas?"

Julio brought the board up again high over his head before Eusebio stuttered, "I mean f-f-f-fifty-four!"

Julio let the board fall again but had to change its trajectory to avoid the fallen man's defensive forearm and settle for a thudding whack to the ribs, "How many? I saw sixty."

"It was 60. It was 60," Eusebio pleaded, fumbling over the ledger and showing Julio the corrected sum.

Julio stood towering over the gaping mouths of the other field hands who had gathered to witness the spectacle. Julio snatched the ledger from Eusebio and declared to all who could hear, "I'll be running the scales now since Eusebio fell and hurt himself. Anyone got a problem with that?"

A murmured ripple went through the crowd as Eusebio scrambled off the truck. Then someone handed Julio their sack and everyone else fell into line.

Anita stood watching with keen interest. Without her realizing it, there was a smile spreading broadly across her lips. This one was different. He had a look. Sure there was lust in his eyes like every other man, but Julio had something else. Determination. "With the right administration, Julio could be someone in this world," Anita thought.

Three weeks later, Anita was pregnant with the first of six children she would have with Julio.

Brothers

It was a big family. So much so that Ama Quina was still having babies when her oldest children started families of their own. The initial significance of this overlapping was that Ama Quina functioned as wet nurse for her grandchildren not long after she had weaned her two youngest boys Sergio and Roy, *El Polaco*—he was called that because his skin was so light he looked Polish. Ama Quina's nueras, daughters-in-law, were not happy about handing over their babies for another woman to nurse, but the young brides' hands were needed in the fields as was the extra paycheck.

The children also learned the importance of work and getting paid. When they were old enough to walk, each child followed the family to the field to pitch in and help with the work. Since the kids were raised so close together and with everyone sharing duties, they did not observe the formalities of family titles as is the custom. The grandparents and heads of the clan, Ama Quina and Apa Cheto, were the only ones to carry a title before their names. For the rest, there were no titles to distinguish one member of the family from the next like tío, tía, primo, prima, hermano, etc. So the children of their second oldest son Julio, Gilbert and Davey, grew up like little brothers to their uncles Checo and el Polaco and called them by their first name instead of tío even though the uncles were years older than the kids. Whenever anyone outside the family commented on this "falta de respeto," Julio would respond, "Es culpa de uno for not teaching them any better." The only way to distinguish which child belonged to each couple was at night when the clan broke up after work and everyone retired to their respective rooms, which were just that, cuartitos, one room shacks that the patron lent the field workers. Following an accident, Julio was laid up in one of these rooms because his hand had been almost severed when it was caught in a spiked press the men were trying to move without the aid of a tractor. His wife, Anita, had pleaded with the doctor to save her husband's hand, and when this did not move the surgeon to action she wrote down his name and was very careful of the spelling because she did not want to make a mistake when her husband woke without his right hand and asked for the name of the man "he must kill for leaving him crippled." The surgery lasted eight hours and there was six months of bed rest before Julio could move around with his arm in a sling. The hand was still attached, swollen and for the time being useless, but the fingers moved under the thick white gauze more and more every day and the burning around his wrist where the spike had bitten and torn his flesh was now almost bearable. He could have enjoyed the time away from the fields had it not been for the constant complaining and quarreling he faced each evening when his wife and kids came back from the campo.

While injured, Julio had to rely on the paychecks of his little brothers, Checo and El Polaco, to sustain his family. But the way Anita told it, she was the only one doing for the family, staying longer in the fields, running back to the cuartito to see to his hand and cooking the midday meal. Julio thought his wife a chiflada who didn't appreciate the help they were getting from Checo and el Polaco. Even Gilbert at ten and Davy only nine years old picked more grapes than she did. This reminded Julio of another of his troubles. Gilbert and Davy had gotten harder to manage for Anita. The boys ran away from her in the fields and preferred to pick the rows next to their uncles Checo and Polaco instead of next to their mother, where she could keep better track of the money they were earning. Anita, Julio thought, just didn't understand boys; it was only natural for them to choose other boys for company over their mother. Julio was at least thankful that Checo and Roy salieron buenos as far as brothers go.

One evening when Anita came home herding the boys in front of her, Julio thought about slipping out of the shack and eating dinner somewhere else. Davy was marching ahead of his mother clutching his pants and howling continuously, his sobs only interrupted by sudden attacks of hiccups. Gilbert walked with a more deliberate pace between his little brother and his mother. His cheeks were streaked with furrowed rows of dust where tears had fallen.

"¿Qué paso?" Julio asked his wife as the group came nearer.

"Tus queridos hermanos," Anita hissed, pushing Gilbert who had all but stopped in his tracks at the sound of his father's voice. "Checo and Polaco were making them fight again. Why don't they fight themselves if they want to see a fight? Why do they have to pick on my babies?"

"Oh, that's how boys play," Julio said, stepping out of the doorway so the group could pass. "You keep calling them babies and they'll never grow up. My brothers are just trying to toughen them up."

Anita turned in the middle of the room. "Toughen them

up? I found them wrestling in the dirt with their pants around their knees. How does that make them tough?"

Julio looked at his boys. Davy was still crying. Gilbert was trying hard to shrink into the furthest corner in the room. "They were just playing."

"Checo and Polaco were poking their little butts with sticks, laughing like idiotas while my babies cried in the dirt." Anita's eyes were rimmed with tears and the veins in her neck looked like they were about to leap out of her skin.

"¿Qué dices?"

"Algo paso, Julio," Anita screamed. "Your brothers did something to my babies."

Julio paced the room like a kenneled dog. His hand throbbed more now than it had all day. Davy had begun a new bout with the hiccups that threatened to drown out Anita's shouting. Gilbert had his face buried in the corner, crying in silence.

"No paso nada," Julio said, rubbing his wrist. "No paso nada."

"Algo paso, Julio. Your brothers did something to my babies."

"No paso nada," Julio shouted. "They're helping us, without their checks we couldn't buy food." He moved on Davy, grabbing him by the arm with his good hand and lifting his bandaged hand in the sling over the boy's head. "¿Verdad que no paso nada?" he demanded from the boy. Davy was silent for a moment then began crying anew.

Anita lunged at Julio, crashing into his bandaged wrist as she screamed, "Poco hombre." Julio winced with pain, released his hold on Davy then shoved Anita to the floor, where she stayed.

Gilbert ran to his mother's arms, but she pushed him away and covered her face to cry. Gilbert kneeled next to his mother sobbing, "No paso nada. No paso nada."

Later, Davy woke in the middle of the night screaming from a nightmare, the first of many. In a couple of weeks, the nightmares came accompanied by incidents of sleep-walking. They tried tying a string to the boy while he slept then attaching the other end around Julio's foot so he could feel if the child got up in the middle of the night. But this only caused the boy to wake up throwing fits, punching, and kicking like a captured savage.

Daytime rivaled the night in its lack of peace. Gilbert and Davy could not get within arm's reach of each other without becoming a tangled mass of kicking feet and gouging fists. The boys' fights caused Julio and Anita to quarrel. The quarrels gave the rest of the camp more to talk about.

Anita and Julio took Davy to Ama Quina for a limpia. Ama Quina rubbed an egg over Davy then cracked it and emptied its contents into a glass of water. The yoke was stained in the center with blood, a true sign of mal de ojo. She took a broom and swept over the boy and then made him hold his head under a towel over a bowl of burning herbs. She frothed the boy in alcohol and wrapped him in sheets. Drying her hands on her apron, Ama Quina said, "Si esto no lo cura, llévalo de aquí."

The camp was talking about Julio's poor luck. His hand all broke up and on top of that a sick kid. But this wasn't all that was being said. Julio's older brother Inez told their sister Lola about how Checo and Roy were joking about making Davy and Gilbert play with their chilitos. Chetito was heard talking with Mel and Rafa about how Checo had told him how he held Davy and the funny garbled noises Davy made when Checo made him kiss Gilbert's pipi. More details leaked out, but no one can be sure what is true and what has been exaggerated when talking about these things.

No one but Checo and Roy—with skin so fair he looked

Polish—could know how surprised Davy and Gilbert looked when they sneaked up behind them as the boys peed. Only Checo and Roy can close their eyes and see the baffled look on Davy and Gilbert's face when Checo asked them, "Whose's bigger?"

"I'm older," Gilbert said.

"But I'm bigger," Davy said still peeing.

"Let's see," Roy said, grabbing Gilbert between the legs. Roy locked Gilbert's hands behind his back and with his free hand reached around and finished pulling the boy's pants and underwear down, all the while shrieking with laughter. Checo had Davy from behind by the elbows, shorts dropped to the knees, grinding the boy's butt into his crotch and yelling, "Look, the little girl likes it."

"Look at Gilbert's pretty chilito," Roy said. "Make him kiss it."

Checo pushed Davy's face between Gilbert's legs. Davy screamed but was muffled by a mouthful of flesh. Gilbert bawled with pain and tried desperately to break free but he was busy trying to get his eyes to close tighter, tighter. When the boys were finally turned loose, they stood facing each other, panting. Davy, feeling a betrayal he could not understand and because he didn't know what else to do, punched his brother in the face as hard as he could. The blow seemed to wake Gilbert out of a trance and he lunged at his little brother knocking him to the ground. They rolled around in the dirt until their mother appeared and Checo and Roy ran off laughing like idiots.

Apa Cheto and the older brothers gathered some money to help Julio move his family to a neighboring ranch that needed a new foreman. His hand was almost fully healed and would be as good as new by the time the harvesting season started again. Two years after that, Julio was able to move his family out of state to Texas where he found an even better job driving a truck for a lumberyard in Houston.

Davy's nightmares became less frequent with every move but never really went away. As time passed, the family talked less and less about the nightmares and more and more about how Gilbert and Davy, even now as young men, couldn't be in the same room with each other without getting into a fight. Everyone agreed that it was very sad that the two boys never learned to get along like brothers.

Four Years Without Sleep

What their mother said: *Yo por eso me regresaba a México para tener a mis hijos. Yo sabía que los Americanos se los iban a llevar a la guerra. Mis hijos no eran ciudadanos Americanos cuando los hicieron pelear. Eran residentes. Pero se los llevaron como sea. Cuando regresaron metieron los papeles y se hicieron ciudadanos. No sé porque hicieron eso. Los gringos ya los habían hecho pelear.*

That's why I always went back to Mexico to have my sons. I knew the Americans would take them to war. My sons weren't American citizens when they made them fight. They were residents. But they took them anyway. When they came back, they put in the papers and became citizens. I don't know why they did that. The gringos had already made them fight.

What their father said: *Les cayeron unas cartas. Eran del gobierno. Y se los llevaron. Primero a Mel. Luego a Rafita. Creo que Rafita tuvo que matar más gente que Mel. Pero no hablamos de esos detalles. Nunca debes de hablar de las vidas que debes.*

They got some letters. They were from the government. And they took them. First Mel. And then Rafita. I think Rafita had to kill more people than Mel. But we don't go into those details. You should never talk about the lives you owe.

What their big brother Julio said: *Lo tenía todo arreglado. Fui a Tijuana y arreglé para que apareciera como si Mel y Rafa habían atropellado a alguien en México y tenían que estar bajo juicio y presentes firmando cada semana para mantener la fianza. Pero no. Mel, que la vieja tenía miedo que perdiera los papeles si no iba. Y Rafa nomás se me quedó viendo y me dijo, "Se me hace que la voy a hacer, carnal." Los dos fueron y vinieron. Ya no eran iguales cuando regresaron. Rafa se hizo mariguano. Cuando llegó Mel, su vieja se fue con su sobrino. Imagínate eso. Tu vieja se fue con el hijo de tu hermano. Ni puedes matar a nadie en esas circunstancias.*

I had everything fixed. I went to Tijuana and put the bribes in so it would look like Mel and Rafa had ran over someone in Mexico and were on trial and had to be present to sign their names every week to maintain the conditions for bail. But no. Mel, said that his wife was afraid that he would lose his papers if he didn't go. And Rafa just stared at me and said, "I think I'll make it, carnal." They were never the same after they came back. Rafa became a pothead. When Mel got back, his woman left him for his nephew. Imagine that. Your woman leaves you for your brother's son. You can't even kill anyone under those circumstances.

Tío Mel's story: It was four years without sleep because first they took me from '65 to '68. And then they took my brother Ralph from '68 to '71. Last two years for each of us was spent in combat. So Mom and Dad didn't sleep for four years worrying over us.

You had to report to the induction center and they give you a physical and swear you in, and that's where the yelling starts. Move here. Move there. Hurry, grunt. But it's all show. They can't do shit to you unless you commit a crime just like on the outside. Then we went to boot camp. And more yelling. They run your ass off. You have to wear a heavy pack. They make you walk through a room with tear gas. At first you get a mask. Then they make you take the mask off, and you have to make it out the other side. You feel like you're choking. Snot flies all over the place. You're eyes water, and you feel like you're going to suffocate. But it passes and it's all more of the show. That goes on for a while. That time don't even really count.

Then we went to Vietnam. Things were different right from the go. We were all American G.I.'s. There was no white, black, Mexican. We were all Yankees. We were on a base at first. Fuckin' kids over there come up to guys and ask to shine their shoes. You put your foot up and they go to work. Then you don't feel the kid cleaning your shoes. And bam! A grenade goes off in the shine box, and a soldier is lying on the ground with a leg blown off. Crazy shit like that. They got whores and bars, and you can play pool on base. But there's always that shit of not knowing who's going to kill you.

We went into the country then. They teach you a few things in Vietnamese like *Dan-gly,* which means stop or something. We never used any of that shit. The closest we came to speaking Vietnamese was saying cocky-sucky mother-fucky. It wasn't like we were there to have conversations. We'd go walking through the jungle, and the next thing you know, Charlie's right in front of you shooting those fucking AK 47's like there's no tomorrow. We had M-16's. A good rifle, but delicate. It would jam up with any little piece of dust. And you're in the jungle with mud up to your ears. I always kept mine clean.

We were crossing a field and came under fire. We all go down and take firing position. In front of me, twenty yards, probably less, I see a helmet, which is rare. Most of the time, it's kids or just villagers shooting at you. They didn't have a real army like us with uniforms and everything. It was just guys and women and kids most of the time. But this guy had a helmet, so he was V.C. regular. He shot at me, and I shot back. I waited for him to shoot back, but he didn't. Then the Sergeant ordered us to advance, and I was able to reach the guy's fox hole. There he was with a little black dot on his forehead. I had got him square. He was a kid, fifteen maybe sixteen. I wasn't much older. I pulled off his helmet and the back of his head spilled out. I only got a second to look down on him and see the big hole where his brain should have been. There's a saying that says, "Either they cry in his house or they cry in mine." And I didn't want anyone back home crying over me. After all, they're sayings por algo.

We did that for a year and a half till I was almost ready to rotate out. We had a village to clear out because the V.C. were coming. But like I said, it's hard because they all look alike, so you don't know if you should shoot one or help one. We had the choppers set down in the L.Z. right on the edge of the village. One of the choppers breaks down and can't take off, but the villagers won't get off. We're pushing and pulling on arms to get these people off the chopper because the V.C. were coming, and we had to get out of there. One of the guys yells for us to get back and then lobs a grenade into the chopper. Most of the people were able to get off when they saw the grenade, but a lot didn't. It made me mad, especially when the guy said, "So? They're just a bunch of gooks." Not little kids and old men and women. Just a bunch of gooks, he said. They busted me down to private from corporal for that fight. It was only $42 difference in pay, but still. Since the bullet only grazed the guy, and because of it getting written up as an accidental discharge, they sent me to Hawaii for R&R instead of the brig. A lot of guys got to visit Hawaii. Your aunt came out and we stayed for two weeks, swimming, lying on the beach. But it was all over for me by then. The war, me and your aunt; it was all over by then. I got a divorce and remarried. I worked at the P.D., the water company, joined a band. I did everything and nothing. I can't sleep. It's hard to concentrate. My head hurts all the time. Every time somebody would offer me drugs over there, I always told them, "No thanks. I have balls." And I do. I still do, but there's something messing with my head and I can't get it to stop. I've gone everywhere and tried everything, doctors, curanderos, priests, but nothing works. I fixed my papers, and even then I couldn't get any help from the V.A.

Tio Ralph's story: They took me right after Mel came home. I did really good on the written part of the test, so they asked me if I wanted to join the Rangers. I figured that if I was going to fight, I had better get the best training I could, so I said yes. They took us down to Louisiana and dropped us into the swamp. There were alligators and snakes all over the place. Then they started shooting. Live rounds. The only order was to survive. I thought, hell, if the training doesn't kill me, nothing will.

As soon as we landed, we were in the shit. I mean right off the plane. They lined us up and told us to grab K-rations and ammo, all you can carry. See, they'll give you all you want of anything you want. You can grab all the food you want or all the bullets you want. At first, a bunch of us grabbed food. Wrong. Get bullets. All you can carry. I used to load up. The bullets probably outweighed me. What do you want food for anyway? You never get hungry over there. All the time I was there, I can't remember feeling hungry. You eat because they tell you to eat and you know you have to, but you're never in a mood to eat.

It's not like in the movies where they all march in all badass. Everyone is scared. Some guys wouldn't even leave the trail to take a shit or a piss. They'd just drop their pants and go right there. And if you're coming behind, you step in that shit. Nobody liked those guys. The ones that didn't give a fuck were those white boys from Tennessee. Oh, and, Kentucky, where your cousin Johnny goes to sell weed. Shit, those white boys got balls. They'll keep shooting no matter what. Les vale madre. I saw one guy get shot in the right arm and all he did was switch his rifle to his left and kept firing. Never missed a beat. See, that's what you have to do, keep shooting. They train us to never retreat and never leave a man in the field. So we dropped fire till our barrels got bent. But the V.C. can't do that. They didn't have supplies like us. The V.C. would hit you then run away. They'd pop up, aim and shoot. They never wasted a shot. They aimed, dropped the safety, and then took their shot. And then they pop the safety back up after they shoot, so they never waste a shot. We would pick guns off of guys after a firefight and they would all be on safety. I swear to God, you could hear the safety's click even in the middle of the shit. Maybe that's how close we were, but I swear you could hear them clicking their guns on and off safety. If one of their guys fell, they left him and came back later. So we started cutting off our insignias and wrapping them around our knives and shoving them up the dead V.C.'s ass so when they picked him up they'd know it was 1st infantry that wasted him.

I got 16 confirmed but I know the number was over forty. The first guy I got was when we came to a river. There were men wading across when I came over the bank. I throw down on one and yell the word for raise your hands, but he would only raise one. I shout two, three times, then start squeezing. He flies back and the other hand comes up with an AK in it. Me iba chingar. It pissed me off to know that he was going to fuck me. I kept firing. I pumped 41 bullets into him. The LT came up to me and asked me to explain why I had shot this man 41 times. I told him that I ran out of clips. He said, 'Good man.' And handed me a full clip and then we crossed the river.

We had to hold our ground. We couldn't take a step back and we couldn't leave until we picked up everybody, even if it was just pieces. I had to bag up a leg, a shoulder, and a head one time. I could never get the eyes closed. We'd make the new recruits carry that shit because half the time it was their fault one of us got wasted. You know what you call a twelve-year-old in Vietnam? V.C. regular. Charlie didn't have to bother with any of that shit. They'd just spring up from the jungle and start firing. You couldn't even tell they were there until the shooting started. That's how good they hid. So we'd drop Agent Orange and burn all the foliage. Two-hundred gallon barrels we'd move around in just our T-shirts. They wouldn't even give us a mask. That's why my lungs are all fucked up. When your Tio Checo was crying because he thought he was going to jail over that coke we were moving, he said he wanted to kill himself. I was in the hospital getting a lung removed. I told him, "Go to my house and tell Francis to give you my gun from the nightstand. Use it on yourself, but first leave a letter donating me your lung, pendejo." Anyway, after we got the leaves all burned off, we could go back in and search for Charlie. But they tunnel in; they build whole cities underground. You got to go in there and get them out. We'd set up ambushes of our own. It was in Laos, or maybe Cambodia, probably both; we laid Claymores along a trail then hit Charlie while they were humping through with supplies. I saw a V.C. get ripped in half. His head and shoulders fell with the sack of rice he was carrying, but his legs kept running for about five paces. That sack of rice would have fed a whole platoon. Eran cabrones los Vietnamese. You had to keep on Charlie all the time. I did all that shit, tunnel rat, explosives, point. Oh, man, point. I did nine and a half months on point. I've never met or heard of anyone doing more. Life expectancy is two weeks on point. I lasted nine and a half months. I should have gotten a Hollywood contract. No one does that. Nine and a half months; I'd like to meet someone else who can say that. But I knew I wasn't going to get it. I don't know how, but I just knew; even when I was getting close to coming back to the world.

You see, the closer you come to the end of your tour, the more you worry about getting wasted. A lot of guys got wasted waiting for the Huey that was going to take them back to the world. So when I'm getting close to the end of my tour, I try not to think about it. Then my Sergeant tells me that we're going out and he wants me on point. When you go out, it's five guys in a line, and you head out in one direction. Ten or twenty kilometers away, another group like yours heads out from the opposite direction. You hump it through till you meet up in the middle or the shit starts, whatever comes first.

I tell Sarge he should put some fresh meat on point; I

was about to be reborn. He said that he knew but that he was pretty sure we were going to meet Charlie that day and he wanted someone with experience on point. I thought about it and knew he was right. The new guys will walk you right in to an ambush. So, we start to hump it, and a few clicks in, I hear chatter and it sounds friendly. I turn to the Sergeant, and I'm pointing my rifle at him now because everywhere you look, you have your rifle drawn and ready to fire. So I got my sling tight and the M-16 waist high when I turn and tell the Sergeant I hear chatter and it sounds friendly. "How far did you say the other group was? Because I hear friendly." Can't be, he says. Friendly was still five clicks out at least, so he sends me back up to check. I take a few more steps and the grass parts and a V.C. with a R.P.G. strapped across his back steps forward rattling off in Vietnamese. Hell, I only weighed 98 pounds, we hadn't showered in weeks. I guess I did look a lot like them.

We both figured it out at the same time. He must've read my face when I realized he thought I was V.C. because he pulled the R.P.G. just as I squeezed the M-16 and side-stepped. The rocket shot by me and blew off the Sergeant's right arm. I got the Silver Star with Oak Leaf Clusters for that one, "For gallantry in action." Leaving my position of cover under fire to aid a wounded comrade. They don't pin medals to your chest like in the movies. They give you a certificate. I asked them what I was supposed to do with it, and the guy told me to take it down to Denny's with a dollar and maybe I could get a cup of coffee.

He wasn't kidding either. When I came back to the world, I landed in San Francisco. The hippies were there at the airport. They spat on me and called me a baby killer. I took off my uniform in the bathroom and left it there on the floor. I walked out of that airport telling myself over and over that that's why we fight, for people to have that freedom. But I didn't believe it then any more than I believe it now.

When I was over there, they would put me to guard whole fields of weed and poppy. I could have helped myself, or scored any number of ways. Over half the guys in my unit were hooked on smack before we even left. I never touched shit while I was over there. I never even smoked a cigarette, much less a joint. When I left the airport in San Francisco, I went and bought my '63 Falcon and a pound of weed with my combat pay. I didn't even know how to roll. Hell, I still don't; I have to use a rolling machine. All the time I was over there, I thought I had to be in my five senses to survive, but I got it backwards. Yeah, man. I had it all wrong.

Lourdes's Birthday

Lourdes sat on her back porch watching her cousins with contempt. Their houses sat back-to-back, and Itta and Suzy were playing under the big tree that was just beyond the six-foot chain-link fence that separated the two back yards. Lourdes could not conceal the disgust from her face. She could only find comfort knowing that her cousins were too immersed in their game that they did not notice Lourdes making herself small between the washer and dryer that sat on the porch with her. Itta and Suzy were making mud pies. And as if playing in the dirt and filth wasn't bad enough, they were feeding the mud pies to that ugly doll they always lugged around with them wherever they went. The doll was a big one that stood around three feet high. Its blond hair was now dark and matted with mud. The doll was missing an arm and naked save for a diaper fashioned out of a bandana that was too dirty to tell what color it had originally been. The doll sat spread legged at the base of the tree receiving scooping handfuls of mud pie. Between bites, the doll would fall over on its side triggering a recorded voice to say, *"I fell, mama."* Every time the doll fell, it would repeat the words in a voice that was meant to resemble that of a child but sounded more like a wounded animal gasping its last sigh, *"I fell, mama."* Once the doll was righted and sitting, it would let out a tattle tale laugh, *"Hahaha Ha Ha."* Lourdes could feel her flesh tighten and break out in goose bumps at the sound but still could not take her eyes off the scene. How could they be so ugly? She asked herself. They were of the same blood. Their father was her father's first cousin, and the men shared the Cortina good looks, dark wavy hair, bulbous nose, full lips hooded by a finely trimmed mustache and a stare to match the walk—the Cortina men all walked like they could own the world but preferred not to be bothered by such trifles. Oh, sure, Itta and Suzy's mother was nowhere near as beautiful as Lourdes's mother, Anita. But still. Her cousins should at least be clean and pretty like her even if they only had half of the good looks Lourdes had. Lourdes knew she was a younger version of her mother and she was equally confident that she was only a few years shy of blossoming into being the staggering beauty that was her mother. Lourdes always proudly held her mother's hand as she walked into Midklif Elementary with the other children and their mothers because she knew her mother era la mas bonita que todas.

Lourdes was sure that all of her father's brothers and cousins were in love with her mother. She knew that in a short time her house would fill with relatives coming to celebrate Lourdes's twelfth birthday and that all the men would be stealing glances at her mother. Anita, even pregnant with her sixth child, could turn every head in any room she entered. Conversations would stop mid-sentence and wives would send dagger-filled stares across the room to their husband who would boldly ignore their better halves for a chance to enjoy a full look at Anita's shapely rear and perky chest topped by the most beautiful smile and wonderful eyes that God had ever created. Lourdes could just imagine how in less than an hour her house would fill with the scent of Three Flowers hair cream and Aqua Velva aftershave lotion. The men would file in wearing their best Guayaberas and their shiniest shoes and line the wall shoulder to shoulder exchanging conversation and bellowing laughter. But Lourdes knew the women would be coming as well.

Her aunts would file in along with the men with their powdered faces and mascara lined eyes that would be bulging inspecting every bit of the room desperately searching for something out of place so as to have something to critique about Anita, aside from the usual, "Yo no se como haya tiempo Anita para estar tan bonita." Lourdes didn't mind that her aunts envied her mother. What she did mind was that without fail, the aunts would all be eager to beg the question, "Ya es señorita, Lourdes?" Since Lourdes's last birthday, her aunts had taken up a vigil for her first period. The truth was that Lourdes had started having periods six months ago but had managed to keep the news hidden from her mother. Lourdes knew that as soon as her mother found out, Anita would have no course of action other than to proclaim the event to her mother-in-law, and from there Ama Quina would make sure everyone found out and that would be the end. Lourdes would no longer be allowed to play outside with the boys or gather around her uncles in the evenings and listen to the stories of the day's work and what the future harvest might bring. She would no longer be allowed to ride in the front of the truck with her father who sometimes let her sit on his lap and steer. She would have to ride in the back with the rest of the women and hear more stories of her cousins starting their periods. Lourdes suffered cramps and could hardly make it out of bed in the mornings and absolutely hated having periods and was very confused when her aunts and grandmother would shake their heads in disapproval when it was announced that one of her cousins had somehow managed to make her period disappear. There were so many questions she had but knew she could not ask. Lourdes was so lost in these thoughts that she did not notice that her cousins and the doll had disappeared from the back yard. Lourdes searched the yard and stood and peered to the sides of the house wondering where they had run off to, not that she cared or anything, but it was strange how they had just vanished like that. The back door opened and Anita poked her head out and said, "Ya tienes que get ready. People are starting to get here already."

Lourdes went into the house and took the dress her mother had made her for her party into the bathroom to change. It was a summer dress with big yellow flowers and spaghetti straps that tied behind her neck holding up the top part of the dress. Lourdes stood in the mirror looking at her small breasts before tying the dress. She dropped the straps and pushed her breast together with her hands and leaned into the mirror to see better. The door opened and she turned to look in paralyzed shock. Halfway through the door was her dad's cousin, Tio Barbarito, the youngest and cutest of all the cousins. For a brief instant he stared back at Lourdes equally surprised, but only for an instant. In a blink, a look of fiendish delight lit over his face and just as quick as the look appeared, he was in the bathroom with Lourdes and across the floor with his hands cupping Lourdes's small breast. Lourdes stood frozen wondering how he could have crossed the bathroom so quickly and would probably still be wondering had her uncle not let out a devilish laugh that prodded Lourdes into action. She grabbed the rest of her dress and tied it behind her neck as she pushed her way past her uncle and out of the bathroom.

Lourdes ran and found her mother in the kitchen scooping fideo into bowls for the guests. "Mom, Tio Barbarito, came into the bathroom while I was in there."

"How many times have I told you that you have to start locking the door? Boys don't knock," Anita said.

"Mom, I hadn't finished putting on my dress and he saw me."

Anita stopped what she was doing and turned and looked sternly at her daughter. "And?"

Lourdes swallowed hard before saying, "He touched my chiches."

Anita clutched Lourdes by the arm with the same firmness that her uncle had grabbed her breast. Anita looked into her daughter eyes and hissed, "Ya vas a empezar? I worked really hard to make you this party." Anita shook her daughter with every word. "I told you. I told you, you have to lock the door." Anita pulled her daughter close to her where they were both eye to eye and said, "Your father will kill him." Anita let loose of Lourdes and made the girl turn around. Anita tightened the straps that held up the dress and sent Lourdes into the living room with a tray full of fideo to serve to the guests.

Lourdes sat in the living room surrounded by her family and yet she felt scared and alone. She sat darting her glances to each face wondering who among them knew she had been touched. She was sure that everyone could tell that she had been touched and was no longer pure just by looking but maybe they knew even more than that. She wanted to know if her mother had said anything to anyone or even worse what if Tio Barbarito was telling everyone how he caught her examining her breasts. Every now and then she would catch him looking at her out of the corner of his eye and she knew that the grin that reminded her of a sheep killing dog was meant for her. Her aunts and uncles smiled and laughed and clapped their hands and slapped their knees but she was sure that everyone knew and that at any moment someone would blurt out the truth and the whole room would turn to her in judgement.

It came time for Lourdes to open her gifts. Aunt Kathy and Tio Rudy gave her a small jewelry box covered in sea shells. Tia Vicenta, and her cousins Erasema and Estela, gave her a brush and mirror set. There were diaries and pen sets and pieces of costume jewelry from other aunts and cousins. And so the gifts went on with the same coming of age theme until there were no more left but the one Itta and Suzy held in their still mud caked hands. The cousins stood before Lourdes—Suzy had snot running out of her nose—holding a big box wrapped half in Christmas paper and the other half in newspaper. Lourdes turned and gave a pleading look to her mother, but Anita only sucked her teeth and hissed, "Andale."

Lourdes took the box and began peeling off the paper. But she was taking too long for Itta and Suzy who were eager to show their cousin the gift they had brought her and they began tearing off the wrapping themselves. Lourdes sat with her mouth open in horror for the second time that day. There in her lap was the dirty doll her cousins had been feeding mud pies earlier. The doll stared up at her with one closed eye under matts of muddy hair. Lourdes grabbed the doll by the only arm it had only to release it again after the doll cried, "*I fell mama.*" Lourdes looked up and around the room and was then drawn back to look at the doll because it had suddenly begun to laugh, "*Hahaha Ha Ha.*" The room exploded with laughter. The doll laughed. Her cousins, aunts, uncles, parents siblings, everyone laughed. But the only laughter she could hear was her uncle Barbarito's. It filled the room and echoed in her head. She grabbed the doll and ran outside and threw it over the fence. By the time she turned to run, her mother had her by an arm and was giving her nalgadas and prodding her back into the house and to her room. From her locked bedroom door, Lourdes could still hear the ring of laughter. She sat in her room too embarrassed to even answer when her cousins came one by one knocking and asking if she was ok through the door. Lourdes was too embarrassed to turn on the light even after the sun went down. She just sat there in the dark full of shame. She was so embarrassed that she would forever remember that day as the most humiliating of her life.

The 4ᵗʰ of July, Mexican Style

It was because of Lourdes. Not that it was her fault in any way. But she was the reason the white boys hung out on the corner when the sun went down. They huddled in a circle across the street from the Cortina's new house in direct view of Lourdes sitting on the trunk of her mom's '77 Ford LTD. Lourdes wasn't doing anything but reading *Teen Beat* with the little neighbor girl, Jill Walker, and talking about the new Z-28 Camaro that Lourdes was going to get for her sweet sixteen that was coming soon at the end of August. She had declined to have a quinceniera when she turned fifteen on the promise that she would receive the car a year later on her sixteenth birthday. The sweltering Houston summer forced the girls in to cut-off Levi shorts and spaghetti strap blouses—and neither would ever wear a bra. They'd get together in the late afternoon when the trunk of the car had cooled down enough for them to sit on it with their backs leaning on the rear windshield and their bare legs—spread ever so slightly—dangling off the trunk. So that's why the white boys were there on the corner, to ogle the girls, and that's why the trouble started.

It could have been innocent enough, neighborhood boys

checking out the girls next door, if it were a different class of white boys. The lanky boys with sandy wire like hair were not of the Heath, Lance, or Justin variety. These white boys were known by monikers such as Smack and Onion, and there was Clyde, and of course Big Red and that punk Jimbo, who collectively called themselves The Animals. Someone from the group found a dog skull and stuck it on a fence post in front of the entrance to the subdivision with a sign that read: This neighborhood run by The Animals. When the sign first appeared, it was taken as a joke given that only Clyde and Big Red, because they were already leaving their teen years, looked like the only two in the group that could fight their way out of a paper bag. They were all in school with Lourdes—except for Clyde and Big Red. Most of the day they spent at the end of the block working on Clyde's '67 Camaro or Big Red's '69 Mustang. But when the sun started to go down, and the neighborhood streets swelled with kids riding bikes and skate boards, the wannabe gang sauntered down the block to the street lamp on the corner across from the Cortina house. They stood around in a circle under the street lamp, slightly rotating so that each member of the motley crew could get a gander at the girls giggling on the trunk of momma's car.

The whole scene, even though often repeated, would have gone unnoticed had it not been the 4th of July. Most days, Lourdes's sharp eye was quick enough to see her father's car round the corner into the neighborhood through the vacant field that banked the outer edge of the Shady Grove subdivision before it turned down her street—giving her enough time to run into her house and change her cut-off Levi's and skimpy blouse for long pants and a long-sleeved shirt. But since it was the 4th of July, Lourdes's older brothers were there with their wives and children. Chemita was down from Dallas with his wife Lisa and their two children, two-year-old Little Joe—but better known as Bouchy, and baby Angelo. Junior was in from California with his new wife, Cindy, and Rueben had his girlfriend Pam over for the day. Lourdes's older brothers were just as strict as their father when it came to how their sister dressed and what she could reveal. But on this day, Lourdes defiantly wore her Gloria Vanderbilt jeans that accented her round butt stunningly and a snug T-shirt that clung to her perky chest for dear life. This uncharacteristic display of fashion boldness was due to the urging of her sisters-in-law.

"If you got it, flaunt it, cuñada."

"You gotta put it out there."

"Don't worry about your brothers, we know how to handle 'em."

Lourdes even had support from her mother who stifled Mr. Cortina's protest over his daughter's outfit with a quick, "Can't I have just one day without hearing pendejadas? It's not like she has anything worth looking at."

It was easy for Lourdes to get caught up in the moment. The whole block was charged with excitement in anticipation of the night's celebration. It was a Friday *and* the 4th of July. The subdivision was outside the city limits, so setting off fireworks was permitted. Chemita had gone to a stand and come back with bags and bags full of bottle rockets, roman candles, kitty chasers, sparklers, black cats, volcanos, and all sorts of other delights that whizzed and whirled then blew to pieces. Lourdes's little brothers, Johnny and Raulito, hopped on their bikes and informed all the neighborhood kids of the cache of fireworks. As word spread, kids poured out of their homes with their own bags of firecrackers and kitty chasers. By 7:00, when the sun was just over the treetops, there had already gathered a swarm of over a dozen kids in front of the Cortina house waiting for the sun to give its final plunge into darkness so they could all let slip their explosive treasure.

Junior had spent the day riding motorbikes with a neighborhood kid, Curtis. Junior had a Yamaha 125 and Curtis rode a smaller Honda. The subdivision was built on the skirt of cow pastures. Junior and Curtis had blazed burns and makeshift ramps all day long and were filthy with mud and cow patties. The bikes were equally muddy and the boys walked them onto the Cortina driveway and commenced to hose them off. Junior was immediately annoyed by the large gathering of kids around the house.

"What the fuck are all these brats doing here?" Junior said to no one in particular.

His next in line brother, Rueben, was leaning his large frame against Junior's Datsun pickup nursing a beer. He looked across the street at the group of older boys and then back to his mother's car where his sister was and said, "They're checking out the scene."

Junior mulled over his brother's words as he finished squirting Curtis's motorcycle free of mud. "You're all set, kid. Get on home now and don't forget to check your oil before you crank it up again."

Curtis pushed the bike down the drive and started crossing the street with Junior lagging a few steps behind. Junior stood at the edge of the drive way squirting the mud off the drive with the hose, but he was only using the occasion to size up the boys who called themselves The Animals.

Rueben called out to his older brother, "Hey, fool, what are you doing? Let's go on a beer run. I'm empty."

Junior turned to answer but instead caught a view of his sister bent over the trunk of their mother's car with her ass toward the street. He was just about to order her indoors when he heard Curtis yell, "Hey, leave me alone."

The boys on the corner had formed a circle around Curtis and his motor bike impeding his progress. The lanky teen called Onion had the bike by the handlebars with the front tire gripped firmly between his legs. The younger kids had stopped their bike riding and skate boarding to witness what would happen next, making the whole intersection crowded with stretched necks and bobbing heads. Smack reached over and pushed on Curtis, trying to pry him away from the motorcycle but Curtis held firm.

"Don't be such a pussy. Let us ride your bike," Smack said bumping his chest into Curtis.

"No. I don't want to."

"Why not? You little punk," Jimbo squealed getting into Curtis's face.

Junior crossed the street and made his way almost unnoticed to where the boys were bullying Curtis. "He said he doesn't want to lend you his bike."

The white boys turned with a start at the sound of his voice but had to search the crowd for the person who spewed the challenge. Junior stood five-six, just a little taller than the average 8th grader riding bikes that afternoon. His puny size masked the tremendous agility and strength that had helped him capture second place in California's state Roman-Greco wrestling competition. Junior made his presence known by stepping forward right into the center of the group. Smack's back got rigid as he turned to square off in front of Junior, "What you gonna do 'bout it?"

The whole sentence hadn't even finished drawling out when Junior savagely landed an overhand right, splitting Smack's upper lip. Smack brought his hands to his mouth and felt his palms fill with blood. He was shocked with pain and the sight of Junior springing in front of all his friends and unloading a barrage of punches. For after hitting

Smack, Junior pounced in front of Onion and bloodied his nose. Onion tripped over the bike's wheel trying to get away. Junior leaped over him and landed in front of Clyde, who stood head and shoulders over Junior. Junior landed a short kick to Clyde's knee cap causing him to bend at the waist and putting his jaw at a perfect angle for Junior to connect. And this he did with stunning accuracy. Clyde fell headlong and would have tasted pavement had his fall not been stopped by Big Red. At the sight of a staggering Clyde, the rest of the group sprinted down the block away from the Cortina house. Clyde and Big Red walked slowly down the connecting street to Clyde's house. Big Red kept looking back over his shoulder and muttering curses. Clyde only turned to see if Lourdes was watching. The younger kids jeered at the fleeing band and rode after them on their bikes. Half way down the block on the street facing the Cortina's house, Jimbo stopped his run and turned toward Junior.

"Fuck you, wetback," he yelled shooting the middle finger. "Come get me, you fucking wetback."

Junior started to sprint down the block but stopped after only a few steps since Jimbo had once again taken flight.

By the time Junior finished washing off his own bike and changing clothes to take Rueben on a beer run, the gang of white boys had made their way around the block and were seated under the big oak on the next corner. The oak was enclosed by a chain-link fence that ran along the ditch in front of the house. The boys leaned their backs on the fence and let their lanky legs stretch out in the ditch. Rueben saw the group as they were driving by before Junior did and was thinking of ways to distract his hot-tempered older brother long enough to pass the white boys without notice, but Jimbo stood up and shot them the bird.

Junior stopped the Datsun and was out of the truck in a

flash but not fast enough to catch Jimbo who had bolted in the opposite direction. Junior got back in the Datsun determined to take chase but found the truck off and missing its keys. Rueben sat grinning in the passenger's seat dangling the keys out the open window.

"You need to settle down. I want a beer and until next year, I need you to get it for me," Rueben said.

Junior pointed down the street and said, "You just gonna take that shit from that punk?"

"Fuck him. He's just a spoiled white boy. Besides, remember what Dad always says: 'You kick one white guy's ass, and soon someone with a piece of paper will show up.'"

"We live here now. We let them get away with this shit now, they'll think they can punk us."

"And the next thing you know, they'll be hitting on Lourdes. I saw what you saw. But fuck 'em. Let's get some beer."

Junior drove slowly out of the neighborhood, brooding. He studied the street and hatched a plan. If the punk was stupid enough to still be on the corner when they came back from getting the beer, he wasn't going to get away again.

On their way back from the store, Rueben was just about to pop the tab on a can of Budweiser when Junior stopped him by putting his hand over the can. "Wait a minute. There they are again. And there's that punk with his back toward us."

"That ain't him. Let's go."

"Yes it is. Get off and stand over there across the street and block him when he tries to run away." Rueben exited the truck cussing and flailing his arms hoping to make enough commotion to startle the white boys. Junior punched the gas as soon Rueben was out of the truck and came careening around the corner then hitting a hard left into the ditch, blocking that route of escape. Jimbo, Onion, and Smack ran off in the opposite direction only to be stopped by Rueben's standing bear charge. He collard Onion and Smack, while the elusive Jimbo tried to back track his way out of Rueben's hulking path. But Junior was on him before he could hardly take a step. Jimbo tucked his shoulder into Junior's chest and tried to block his way past, but Junior only had to grab the white boy by the shoulders and brace his leg in front of Jimbo. A half turn and Jimbo was on his back trying to scurry up the ditch with his palms and the feet like a backward crab. Junior made a skipping motion toward the downed boy and kicked Jimbo square in the nuts. The boy writhed in pain, clutching his ball sack. Junior smiled. He stood over Jimbo and let his body go limp like a string-less marionette. Juniors sinking knees connected just below the exposed abdomen, knocking all the air out of Jimbo. Once that he saw that Jimbo was helpless, Junior pinned his knees against Jimbo's shoulders and sat on his chest. Then in a seesaw rhythm, Junior pummeled Jimbo into an unrecognizable pulp of flesh. Both eyes blackened, with the left bloody and shut. A split nose and lip that flowed profusely sent a crimson streak down Jimbo's shirt. Junior stood gleefully as he watched the boy run away but not as fast as before since he had to stop every few steps to spit out more blood down his shirt and cry.

"Got damn it, you did it now," Rueben told his older brother on the way home. "You shouldn't have fucked him up so bad. A few slaps would have been enough. You didn't have to go all Marvin Hagler."

"Fuck that punk. And fuck those other big bastards too. I'll kick all their asses."

"Did you see how I stopped those other two pendejos?"

"No, I didn't see shit. I was busy knockin' the shit out that punk."

"You could've at least shot a glance. I was magnificent."
Rueben hastily unloaded the beer and made his way indoors where he was determined to remain for the evening, fireworks be damned. Junior followed suit and took a seat in the living room next to his pregnant wife. Neither mentioned what had just happened.

Outside, Chemita was getting bolder and bolder with the pyrotechnics. He had six pop bottles lined up loaded with bottle-rockets and roman candles in alternating sequence. He lit the row and then put a match to a volcano and a strip of black cats. The whole intersection lit up and erupted in hisses fizzles sparks and bangs. The children cheered and begged for more. Chemita was only too happy to oblige. He grabbed the bags of fireworks and began searching for his next fiery delight. While he had his head buried in the bags, no less than six Harris County Sherriff cruisers with lights flashing came to a purposeful halt in front of the Cortina house blocking every form of exit. The cops were out of their cruisers, night sticks in hand, when Chemita screamed "Honest officers, that was the last one." Chemita instinctively put his hands up over his head but forgot to put the bags of fireworks down, making his plea sound all the more ridiculous.

"We don't give a damn about that," one of the cops said. "We're looking for Julio Cortina Jr. You him?"

"No," Chemita said still shaken. "That's my little brother. He's inside."

"Then that's where were going." The cops marched soldier like up the Cortina's walk.

Ruben poked his head out, and the lead cop sprang forward and jammed his foot in the door while pulling Rueben out of the house. "You Junior Cortina? You must be. You fat ass Mexican."

"Nah, hell no. I'm his little brother. Junior's inside."

Johnny and Raulito had run inside ahead of the cops and were crowding the hallway along with the baby Bouchy and the sisters-in-law. Junior appeared at the end of the hall and the cop with the reddest neck marched directly toward him not stopping even when baby Bouchy stood in front of him pointing up and peeping, "Cops, cops, cops." The peace officer just stomped right over the child. Johnny protested, "Hey, didn't you even see the baby in your way?"

The cop without looking back over his shoulder simply replied, "Nope." He stood before Junior Cortina and leveled his night stick at Junior's chest. "You're Junior?"

"Yup."

"You're the punk who beat the shit out my boy?"

"You raised that pussy?"

The cop brought up his night stick and would have let it come down hard had he not been distracted by the sudden flash of light. It was Mrs. Cortina, Anita, snapping pictures with a Kodak 110 camera. "There's not a mark on him. And I got you next to him on film. If one hair is out of place when he reaches the station, I'll have your house. I'll have all your houses."

The hallway swelled with more and more cops pouring in from their cruisers. Now there were eight cop cars with lights flashing in front of the Cortinas' new home. Mrs. Cortina kept lighting up the hall with flashes and warnings of, "And I got you on film. And you. Just one hair, please, and I'll have everything you own." An older officer smiled and said, "Hey James, your boy got his ass kicked by a flyweight."

This sent the rest of the cops in an about face out the door but not without comment, "You should teach your boy to fight."

"Yeah, James. I had dogs on the grill that are burnt by now. Shit, just 'cause your son's a sissy."

The officer they called James cuffed Junior and led him to the cruiser. Junior looked back at his parents and siblings before having his head shoved down and forced into the backseat.

"Don't worry, we'll be right behind you," Anita said, still snapping pictures with the Kodak. She had run out of film long ago.

Mr. and Mrs. Cortina spent the next three nights sitting in the waiting room at the Harris County PD till Monday morning when they could post bail and take their boy home. Anita Cortina repeatedly berated the desk clerk demanding to speak to the chief or whomever else was running this circus, not the clowns. She made loud calls on the payphone to nonexistent lawyers and was vocal about hearing that LULAC and other civil liberties associations had already been contacted and that her boy's case was soon to hit the media. The little slivers of sleep she allowed herself were filled with images of her disfigured boy emerging from the big brown door that led to the detention cells, broken and bloody. She stirred in restless slumber calculating the lawyers' take in the lawsuit and woke with a start at the thought of the injustice of what attorneys could charge a grieving mother.

Junior came out from behind the big brown door in cuffs. A burly guard uncuffed him at the door and directed him to a nearby window. The clerk behind the glass slipped him a large manila envelope containing his belt, wallet, and shoe laces. Aside from dark circles under his eyes from lack of sleep, Junior did not look the worse for wear. Anita sucked her teeth and brought down the camera. She locked her arm around Junior's shoulders and led him out of the station, asking under breath as they started to walk, "Did they rape you? It's ok to tell me."

Junior looked at his mother in slack-jawed horror and shook his head. Mr. Cortina stood as his wife and son exited the waiting room. He took in the names of the men on duty just as he had done for the past three nights. He did not need to study the station too much. He had seen enough of the inside of jails to figure out pretty quickly how the outer offices worked. His son was being charged with assaulting a minor. A just turned twenty-one-year-old beating the crap out of a seventeen-year-old white boy was going to cost a bundle to be reduced to disorderly conduct. The fact the boy's father was a cop was going to give the lawyers leverage to up their fee. Mr. Cortina knew that the boy's father had endured taunts. A trial would cause testimonies and missed days of work, delayed hearings, and more and more taunts from the other cops for the boy's father. Julio Cortina mulled his son's chances and figured he could get him off with probation or even time served. But it would cost. And he would pay.

The legal aspect of the situation did not bother Mr. Cortina as much as the other ramifications that now concerned his new home. The boys who hung out in front of his house were out of school. They had nothing better to do than saunter around the neighborhood brooding for payback. Mr. Cortina knew white people. Julio Cortina knew that the fight in their new neighborhood would not go away with a few hearings and fines.

The night they brought Junior home, the Animals took turns racing up and down the street in Clyde's or Big Red's cars, yelling obscenities and throwing beer cans and bottles. Mr. Cortina stood in his front yard and silently put to memory the cars and their occupants. The second night, the vengeful crew threw another beer bottle but this one full of gasoline. The Molotov cocktail exploded near Junior's Datsun and sent up yellow flames that divided the darkness to silhouette Mr. Cortina's steady frame leveling his Colt .38 Super and emptying a full clip at the fleeing vandal's car.

The raids stopped for a few days. Just long enough for the Cortinas to let down their guard. It was late and the house had been dark for hours. A car drove slowly in front of the Cortina's house and fired two shots from an open window. One of the bullets hit the white shutter that skirted the living room window. The other hit just above the front door.

Julio Cortina sprang out of bed and had his hands on the Ak-47 he had propped against the wall. Mrs. Cortina was even faster. She shot out of her room and was busy going room to room pulling her children out of their beds and forcing them to lie on the floor. Johnny doubled over and started to wretch when he hit the floor. Anita Cortina lifted her son by the hair and dragged him to the bathroom.

Julio Cortina was outside and in the middle of the street with the AK-47 leveled at a pair of fast moving taillights. The car rounded the corner before he could get a shot off. He ran back into his house and down the hall stopping only at the open door of the bathroom where his wife had an end of a belt in each hand and her knee braced on Johnny's back forcing the boy to finish vomiting, "You're not going to stain my new carpet." Mr. Cortina stood with the AK-47 pointed toward the ceiling in the doorway and poked his chin at his wife.

"He's just scared," she said a little flustered. "Why haven't you shot anyone?"

Johnny held out his finger and waved it back and forth trying to tell his dad that he wasn't afraid but Julio Cortina was already down the hall with the rifle stuck out his bedroom window. The room filled with the smell of gunpowder and the night split open to the fire spewing from the machine gun. Mr. Cortina emptied a clip and fixed in another and sprinted for the front door. He met his sons Junior and Rueben, who were each carrying handguns, in the hallway and ordered them to the cars. Junior and Rueben hopped into the Datsun while the senior Cortina got into his Marquis, each leaving in the opposite direction. Mr. Cortina sped down the block toward Clyde's house while Junior and his brother rounded the block. Almost at the corner, they blocked a car. All the Cortina's came out guns leveled at Big Red's '69 Mustang. The doors flew open and began spewing teens. Junior and Rueben, bent kneed and with guns grasped with both hands, pointed their weapons at each fleeing kid as they stumbled out of the car and down the street. Mr. Cortina reached into the driver's side and grabbed a handful of crimson locks and pulled Big Red from the vehicle. He threw him on the ground and shoved the AK-47 in Big Red's face. "You fuck with my family," Mr. Cortina said in broken English. Red cried and Julio Cortina leaned into the rifle.

Only a couple of times in his life had Julio Cortina wanted to kill someone as much as he did that night. He kept the AK-47 in Red's face a long time, long enough for the windows of the now awake houses on the block to light up. He ordered his sons back to their house and kicked Red in the shin before he got back into his car. It was over.

Julio Cortina moved his family out of their new home before the sun came up the next day. They lost the deposit and all the months of mortgage they had paid into their new home. They rented a two story home in an upscale neighborhood in the Cyfair school district. But Mrs. Cortina secretly drove her daughter back to her old school every day.

Mr. Cortina busied himself selling his trucks and canceling his hauling contracts. He had thought long and hard about being run out of his home at gunpoint. He thought about the years he spent picking 400 pounds of cotton a day. He pondered on the long days and nights managing the dairy for the Swedes in California. He thought about running himself ragged all over Houston delivering lumber in his truck so he could buy another and then another and would have a fleet if given the chance. He thought about all these things and decided he couldn't win like a white man, and that it was stupid to think that he could. He gathered all the money he could and bought guns and took them down to Mexico and sold them for three times their worth and discovered other things he could buy and sell for a ridiculous profit. He never did an "honest" days' work ever again.

He kept his promise and bought his only daughter a brand new Z-28 Camaro for her sixteenth birthday. Lourdes used her new car to drive back to her old neighborhood and get pregnant by one of the white boys who had shot at her house.

How It All Started

It was Johnny who first recognized the killers sleeping in his living room. It was a Saturday, and he had gotten up early to beat his siblings to the last bowl of cereal and to watch the Super Friends. He recognized the men from the yellow *Alarma* magazine his father had brought home. Johnny stifled a gasp and crept into his parent's room. He slid his hand under his father's pillow and pulled out a nickel plated .38 caliber Colt Detective Special. Julio Cortina woke with a start when he felt his son's hand pull the gun from underneath his pillow. The boy turned to his father with a reassuring gaze.

"The men from the magazine are in our living room. I'm going to shoot them before they wake up and kill us all."

Julio Cortina snatched the gun from his son's hand and wondered whether he should slap his son or praise him. He laughed.

"Don't worry, mi'jo. It's just El Chaparro and my compadre Lolo," his father said getting out of bed. Julio Cortina slipped into his pants and stuffed the .38 Special into his waistband and took his son by the hand and walked him to the living room. The men sleeping on the coach and recliner snapped out of their slumber when Julio turned on the T.V.

El Chaparro sprang from the couch and bent over to look little Johnny in the eye. "This isn't Raulito, he's too big. You must be Johnny."

Julio said, "He was about to come in and shoot you had I not woken up."

Lolo pulled the recliner down and said, "You should have let him. He would do us all a favor."

El Chaparro laughed and picked up the boy and whirled him around saying, "That's right, Chato. You're growing up right. Shoot strange men. It's better for everyone."

Mrs. Cortina came out of her room tying her robe. "Shoot him. Kill them. That's all you can tell a boy? Let's have some breakfast before you teach my son how to be a pistolero."

El Chaparro put down the boy and exclaimed, "Anita, how is it that you get more beautiful when all of us just get older."

"I take care of myself and I don't run around beating people to death," Anita put her hand on el Chaparro's shoulder. "Ay, Chorty, why'd you have to beat that man to death? Now how's he going to pay you."

El Chaparro followed behind Anita to the kitchen. "He didn't owe us any money. We were just trying to get information from him."

"It wasn't even about money?" Anita's eyes grew wide. She threw up her hands in exasperation and started breakfast.

El Chaparro turned to anyone who would listen. "It was just a bit of police work gone bad. The fucker was a god damn creep. Now that he's dead, he's suddenly become el pinche Papa."

Julio bent over and faced his son eye to eye, "Vivos no valen madre pero muertos son una bronca que nunca se va."

The boy shook his head knowingly even though he did not fully understand the words. He committed his father's words to memory just the same.

The rest of the children flooded out of their rooms and took up spots in the living room and kitchen table. The men sat facing each other. El Chaparro was giving instructions to which Julio nodded and occasionally looked up to his wife who was hovering over the scene with a pot of coffee in her hand.

"You're going to have to talk to the D.A.," El Chaparro said. "And the M.E. Now watch those pinche doctors, eh. They're always trying to play the righteous, but they're just as crooked as the rest of us. He'll have to sign off that the guy died from a heart attack or something that he had before the interrogation."

"Sí, sí, sí," Lolo chimed in. "And that the bruises came from a fall or something."

Julio rose from the table when he saw his wife head back to their room. Anita was waiting just inside the door and grabbed him by the arm and forced his gaze into hers. "You're going to Mexico to fix this for them, aren't you? What about my cousin and his deal? You said you were going to do it. Have you chickened out? Don't be afraid. If I were a man I wouldn't be afraid."

"It's nothing," Julio reassured. "You heard them. Put the bite on a doctor and a lawyer. Like those two aren't going to take any money."

"And who's going to put up all this money?" Anita said through clenched teeth.

"They are of course." Julio looked into the mirror and pulled his comb and ran it through his hair. "They also have to give me for expenses, too. And I got everything set up to do your cousin's deal too. Ya te dije. I got it all covered."

Anita's look softened. "And you'll skim some of the bribe money, right? You aren't just going to do the favor, right?"

Julio took his wife by the arms and brought her into to him. "Don't worry. I have other business to attend down in Reynosa anyway and these guys and their problems just paid my way down there."

"And you're going to leave me some money for the bills and my things, right?" Anita said burying her head into her husband's chest.

Julio Cortina left for the border after breakfast. He packed enough clothes for a week even though he only planned to stay away for a day or two. He traveled south down highway 281 and made a dogleg to Corpus Christi before heading to the border. He found Anita's cousin Jaime pacing nervously in front of his house.

"These men are dangerous people, Julio," Jaime stammered. "What are we going to do if something goes wrong?"

"What could go wrong? They have the money and the means to get the junk here. The merchandise is loaded and already flying to the spot on the highway they told me, and I'll meet it there in an hour."

"Yeah, it will be there in an hour. They're closing down a section of highway and dropping a plane loaded with pot right on 281." Jaime was almost at the brink of tears. "What if the law finds out?"

Julio got back in his car laughing. "Who do you think is closing down the road for us? The cops that's who. What could possibly go wrong?"

Julio Cortina had the whole operation plotted in his mind. He would drive down to Rivera and cross over to Highway 281 to Falfurrias and the checkpoint. A few miles north of the checkpoint and a dozen miles south of the town of Premont on a strip of about seven miles where the brush was extremely thick, the Cessna would land. Out of the brush would come Militon and Neto El Australia with the gas tanks. They would unload the 580 pounds of weed off the Cessna while the pilot refueled. The truck would be loaded and on county roads in a matter of minutes. Once loaded and off the main road, it was just a matter of hitting FM 285 back to Rivera and then it was straight to Robstown, and then Corpus Christie and from there every other city was payday after payday.

He drove until he saw the flashing lights of a state trooper cruiser blocking the northern flow of traffic. He passed a line of cars waiting at the roadblock and exited his car when he got to the front of the line. He walked up to the state trooper wearing mirrored Ray Ban Aviators.

"I'm the guy," Julio said.

"I hope your boy is on time," the trooper said.

They both looked up and saw a white with green striped Cessna approaching overhead. "My guys are always on time," Julio said relieved.

"Go on through and leave our package with my partner on the other end." The trooper busied himself holding up a menacing hand to another car that was approaching the roadblock. Julio drove to where the plane had landed and received a briefcase from the pilot. A truck with a camper approached from the opposite end of the road block and two men got off and started transferring the contents of the Cessna into the camper and then boarded the truck and made a U-turn and sped off. Julio handed the briefcase to the trooper waiting on the other end of the roadblock.

"They're finished," Julio said and drove on. In his rear-view mirror he could see the trooper pulling his cruiser off the road and the traffic resumed. He made another U-turn in Premont and headed south to the Valley.

He crossed into Reynosa via the Hidalgo Texas bridge and made some phone calls. He hung up from a call to Nuevo Laredo in good spirits. The man he was waiting to kill would be out of jail the next day. He had believed that he would have more than a few hours to prepare but the sooner the better he thought, al mal paso dale prisa. He would have to find another car. He had planned for this but the car he had planned on using had expired plates and he did not want to risk a traffic stop. He drove to his sister's house and used her phone and set up meetings for later that day with the D.A. and a doctor. He told his sister that he was taking her car for a day or two and filled her hand with a wad of bills that silenced any protest she could have mounted. He spent the rest of the day filling the hands of the D.A. and the Medical Examiner with crisp hundred dollar bills. The fix was in. He had nothing to do now but drive to Nuevo Laredo and wait.

The next day, Julio waited for hours outside La Loma prison on the outskirts of Nuevo Laredo. He had not eaten since the previous day and his hunger was making him cranky. He talked to some taxi drivers and told them not to take any fairs unless he gave the ok. One of the taxi drivers protested and Julio slapped him hard across the face. The man jumped in his cab and drove away. Julio turned to the other drivers and gave them each a twenty-dollar bill that the men took without question. When the man Julio was waiting for exited the prison he could not find any means of transport to take him from the prison. Julio did not notice the man until he saw him from behind. His chest swelled at the sight. It was him. The same man who would not turn to face him so many years ago when Julio was hoisted up by his big brother Inez to peer through the bars covering the cell window at the jail in Los Ramones. This was the man who had killed his grandfather. It could be no other.

Julio let the man walk until there was nothing ahead or behind him but road. Julio pulled over and stuck his hand under the seat. He pulled out a small tape recorder and pushed the buttons to where it would record. He righted himself and set the car in motion. He drove past the man and edged to the side of the road. He watched the man approaching through the rearview mirror. Julio took a deep breath and told himself to stay calm. The thirty-year wait would soon be over. The man peered in through the passenger window and said, "Could you give a man a ride, Señor?"

Julio smiled showing all his teeth. "Jump in, amigo. I can take you where you need to go."

The man took the seat next to Julio with a sigh. "Everyone thinks it's a good day when someone gets out of prison, but now I have to find a place to stay and a way to live. I couldn't even get a taxi to take me out of there. How am I supposed to find everything else I need?"

Julio looked mildly surprised. "So you just got out? How much time did you throw?"

"Thirty years give or take a week."

"That's a long time. What'd you do?"

"I killed a man."

"It must've been someone important for them to give you thirty years for it."

"He wasn't anybody special. That's just what Mexico gives for murder."

Julio brought the back of his right hand hard across the man's mouth knocking him back into the seat. He grabbed the man from the back of his head and slammed his face repeatedly into the dash board. When the man bowed his head and the blood flowed from his nose, Julio pulled his .38 and forced him out of the car. The man swayed in the wind that was blowing across the road and looked like he would fall, but he held his ground. He took a deep breath and wiped his face of blood. "You're him aren't you? You're the boy from the jail that night they caught me. It's been thirty years. I can't believe you're here."

"Do I look like a boy? Did you think I'd forget? You killed my grandfather with his own bullets. No, señor. I do not forget things like that."

"I had hoped you found God or that maybe you'd get hit by a truck."

"I've been very careful. Now, empty your pockets."

The man took out a few crumpled bills and some worn looking credentials and a crisp sheet stating that he had been released from prison after serving his term. Julio leveled his gun at the man and said, "No te hagas pendejo. I know you have a shiv or something tucked away somewhere. Let's have it."

The man fumbled around his waistband and pulled a five-inch pocket knife out. The man stared longingly at the knife and held it in front of Julio's face in desperate defiance. The man sucked his teeth before throwing the knife to the ground at Julio's feet. Julio picked up the knife and unfolded the blade. He tested the sharpness with his thumb and smiled. "You would have liked to have used this, wouldn't you?"

"If I had gotten to it first, another rooster would be crowing right now."

"Tell that to Satan when you see him." Julio took a step forward and brought his left hand holding the knife out and slashed. The skin under the man's chin opened up with a gurgling sound. He clutched at his neck and staggered. Julio lifted the knife again and stabbed the side of the man's neck sending a stream of blood squirting crimson all over Julio's guayabera. The man fell lifeless at Julio's feet. His neck bent in an impossible position. Julio stood over the man hoping there would be more, but nothing stirred. The wind itself had ceased and not a sound could be heard but Julio's labored breath as he hoisted the body into the trunk of his sister's car. He drove to Reynosa and stopped before entering the town along the banks of the Rio Bravo. Julio slid the body into the murky green waters and watched it roll then sink with the current. He'll float soon enough Julio thought.

Julio drove to his sister's house and changed clothes. He left his sister's car at her house and drove away in his own. He drove across the international bridge and straight to Corpus Christi where he picked up a brown paper bag full of cash. His cut from the load that landed on the highway. In the early morning hours of the next day, Julio arrived to his house in Houston. He told Lolo and el Chaparro that the fix had worked and that they could go home now. The men wasted no time in collecting their things and leaving for the border with much thanks and we'll see you soon. Julio crept into his bedroom and gently nudged his wife awake. "Come here," he said and walked back to the now empty living room. He handed Anita the bag and she let the contents spill to the floor in front of her. The stacks of bills swallowed her ankles.

"What's this? Is this ours?"

"All ours, mi amor," Julio said beaming with pride. "We dropped a Cessna right on the highway and this is my cut."

"A Cessna? You got this from an itty-bitty Cessna? Why didn't you land a jumbo jet, or a box car full, or hell, why not the whole train? If you could get this for just a Cessna, imagine what a big plane would bring? Why are men so stupid?" She collected the money and began arranging the stacks on the coffee table. "I wish I were a man. I wouldn't be afraid. I'd show you and everybody how it's done."

She was still complaining when Julio picked up the phone to call his father to tell him that his grandfather's death had been avenged.

In Reynosa, Julio's sister opened her trunk and saw it covered in blood. "Julio must have killed a chivo and didn't even put plastic down. Look at this mess," she said shaking her head. She slipped behind the wheel and noticed the tape recorder sitting next to her in the seat. She pressed rewind and then after a moment pressed play. "Let's hear some corridos this morning," she said. She immediately recognized her brother's voice but was at a loss as to who the other man was. She bent her neck and listened with all her might. Suddenly she slammed her breaks causing a cascade of screeching tires and honking horns, but she could no longer move or do anything but yell at the top of her voice, "Oh my God. Oh my God. Julio, what have you done?"

Acknowledgments

I would like to give special thanks to my family: my parents, grandparents, aunts, uncles, cousins, siblings and all the strayed broken and travel weary people who came into our lives, for the ability to tell a story. I can remember countless hours of sitting quietly in the kitchen pretending to eat or in the living room pretending to watch TV while the grown-ups talked in hushed tones and whispered gasps of astonishment about things that should not have been known and that should never be repeated. I used to linger about trying to go unnoticed while the elders of our clan laid out our family's darkest secrets until I blurted out, "But why...?" I would then get yelled at and ordered out of the room with Mom saying, "You're always hearing things you shouldn't and then you can't just be quiet; you have to say something." My father would ask, sometimes with pride but oftentimes with resentment, "Why are you always interested in these things that happened to us?" They were all great storytellers who were blessed with a special ability to recognize significance. From my family, I learned why stories are told even when they shouldn't be. For this, I will always be grateful.

About the Author

Juan Ochoa is the author of *Mariguano*, a novel set in the drug trafficking world of the Texas/Mexico border circa the 1980s. His short stories and essays appear in numerous journals. He teaches writing at South Texas College in McAllen. Ochoa is a licensed Mexican lawyer with an MFA in creative writing. He is currently writing the final volume in the trilogy, *El Penal*.

www.ingramcontent.com/pod-product-compliance
Lightning Source LLC
Chambersburg PA
CBHW011758010726
47497CB00013B/3267